On the Outside

Siera Maley

*For my brother, who wants to know when I'll tell him
my pseudonym so that he can read my books. Never,
Brother. Never. Just kidding; maybe someday.*

Prologue

It was a hot day in Jonesburg, Washington as the summer of 2012 drew closer to an end, and I felt it on the back of my neck as I peddled past the next two houses down from my own, my dark brown hair pinned to the top of my head in a messy bun to help keep myself cool.

The heat made the trip to the creek feel longer, and I was sweating heavily by the time I finally dumped my bike in Evan's driveway. From there, I jogged through his neighbor's backyard. The line of trees beyond promised shade, and the knowledge that I'd soon be able to splash water over my face and neck spurned me on.

Leaves crunched beneath my feet as I ran through the woods, and so Evan and Riley heard me coming.

"Kayla!?" I heard Riley shout. I whistled back, long

and high-pitched – a special signal we'd created when we'd first started coming here – and heard laughter when the sound faded.

Evan was ankle-deep in the creek when I arrived, his pants rolled up to his knees and his shaggy blonde hair sticking with sweat to the back of his neck. Riley was tucked under the small shelter we'd built a year ago with her dark hair pinned up like mine. Evan's dad helped build houses for a living, and he'd let us have the spare wood he kept in his garage in addition to a hammer and a box of nails, so we'd built something to sit in with all of it. It didn't look great, but it did have a floor and a roof to provide shade, and that was what mattered. That, and the fact that we'd done it all by ourselves.

I took a moment to dip one hand into the creek and then dab myself on the back of the neck with the cool water.

"What took you so long?" Evan asked me a few seconds later as I squeezed into the shelter with Riley. She grinned at me and tangled half of our fingers together. My pinky and ring finger were linked with her index and middle fingers, and we shared a look as Evan climbed out of the creek. For a moment, I forgot he'd asked me a question. Riley squeezed my fingers with hers as Evan tried to get my attention. "Hello?"

"Oh, I had to eat lunch," I finally answered. I bent my legs, pulling my knees up to my chest so that Evan could inch himself into the shelter in front of me. "How long have you been waiting?"

"Just around ten minutes," Riley answered for him.

Evan sighed and leaned back, resting his head at Riley's feet. As he stared up at our makeshift ceiling, he asked, "Can you believe it? We start *high school* tomorrow."

"Everyone makes it sound so scary," said Riley, "but I think it could be fun."

"Nicole likes it," I told them. My older sister had just finished the tenth grade, and she'd loved every minute of it. A senior boy had asked her to Prom a few months ago. I wondered briefly if I'd ever be that lucky.

"But Nicole's pretty and popular," Riley replied. "And she wears makeup and nice clothes. Kayla, you're cute so you'll do fine, but all I have going for me are a pair of Converses and a skateboard."

"What are you talking about? You're both pretty," Evan cut in, nudging Riley's leg with his fist.

Riley and I shared another look, and then we gasped, pressed a hand to our chests, and let out a joint, "Awwwww!"

"Shut up," Evan mumbled. I could see his cheeks going red. I think that was mostly because of Riley. I caught him staring at her sometimes, but his crush seemed entirely one-sided, and I was thankful for that. Our trio wouldn't be the same anymore if two of us ever started dating. "Fine, you're both hideous. Better?"

"Much," agreed Riley. She reached out to grab his hand and then pulled him up into a sitting position. "Hey, we have to agree on this, okay?"

"On what?" I asked, and she shot me a look that told me not to interrupt.

5

"We're starting high school tomorrow. Everyone talks about how it's super important, and the teachers are stricter, and it's gonna decide who we are and what we do with our lives and all that. Like, it changes you and stuff. But you guys have been my best friends since I was six, and I kind of don't want to lose that."

"Of course you won't lose us," said Evan. "We'll probably have tons of classes together, and even though we'll make other friends, we'll just introduce them to all of us and we can all be friends with them. Just like we did with Remi and Vincent."

"But they're not going to our high school," I reminded him. "So we probably won't get to see them anymore."

"I know," he said, "but we can find more people we all like. And we'll all eat lunch together. Things don't have to change just because we're going to a bigger school."

"So we all agree. No matter what happens, and no matter who we become, we'll always be best friends," said Riley. "Deal?" She untangled her fingers from mine and offered a pinky up in the middle of the three of us.

"Deal," Evan and I agreed, and then linked our pinkies with hers.

Chapter One

"C'mon Knights!"

Next to me, Vanessa had both arms in the air and was shaking the pompoms gripped in her hands, trying to pump up the audience in the stands. We shared a grin and I joined her, facing the crowd as a whistle sounded. I knew that meant that the ball was back in play. There were less than fifteen seconds left on the clock, and we were down by a single point. "Knights fans, let them hear you!"

The crowd erupted into a roar, first in response to Vanessa, but then they grew louder and several of them shot to their feet, pointing to something behind us. Vanessa and I spun around with the rest of the squad as the voice of Vice Principal Hunter – the announcer for the game that would decide the state basketball champions for the season – boomed across the gym. "And with six seconds left on the clock, Carver has stolen the ball! He's got a clear run to the hoop!"

Vanessa let out a squeal beside me and gripped my arm as I, wide-eyed, watched Josh sprint down the court and all the way to the basket, where he laid the ball up into the hoop. The buzzer sounded, the Knights' score on the scoreboard ticked from a 51 up to a 53, surpassing the Sharks' 52, and the gym erupted into cheers. The rest of the team crowded Josh, jumping up and down, and he was hoisted into the air.

"Josh Carver has done it! Knights win! Knights win!"

"Every girl in school is going to be jealous of you," Vanessa said into my ear, and just as the words left her lips, Josh motioned for his teammates to let him down and then rushed over to me. Vanessa let me go and shot me a grin as he wrapped his arms around me and hoisted me into the air. I laughed and cupped his cheeks in my hands, kissing him, and he tucked his face into my neck when we broke apart.

"Oh, man. I can't believe I did it," he said, his voice muffled. I squeezed him tighter. He'd talked endlessly about wanting to finally win a championship, and this had been his last chance to do it. In just a few short months, he'd be graduating and heading off to college in California. I'd hardly see him after that. I was still a junior.

But this wasn't the time to think about that. Now it was time to let him celebrate.

***

Josh drove me home after the game rather than letting me take the bus with Vanessa, despite my arguing against it. "You should be out celebrating," I told him in the car, and he shook his head.

"The guys and I are going out later tonight. Don't worry about it."

"You sure?"

"If I wasn't sure, I wouldn't be driving you," he laughed. "But are *you* sure you wanna turn in for the night? I could, uh, rent us a hotel room..."

"You're already doing that for Prom," I reminded him, avoiding the question.

"Yeah, I know. But I'd do it twice, if you wanted."

"You should be with your team. Go celebrate with them." I prodded him in the arm. "Just don't touch any girls. I know you'll be a famous college player soon, but try to keep me in your thoughts until then, alright?"

He laughed again. "C'mon, Kayla. I love you. Besides, they only aired the game on the local channel. No one probably watched it. And if they did, they were probably just like, 'Who's that *really* hot chick that guy's celebrating with?'"

"Shut up." I swatted at his arm, beaming, as he pulled up in front of my house. "And come here." I tugged him toward me for another kiss, then turned to get out of the car. "I'll see you at school Monday, alright?"

"Of course. Bye, babe."

"Bye."

I shut the door and watched him drive away, then

9

retrieved my cell phone from my purse. I typed out a text and then sent it.

Mom was waiting inside for me on the couch, and leapt to her feet to come give me a hug as soon as I walked through the door. She adored Josh almost as much as I did. "Oh, honey! I saw the whole thing!"

"It was so much fun," I told her. "Vanessa was freaking out afterward."

"I expected you to stay out late celebrating," Mom replied. "Is everything alright?"

"Yeah, it is. It's just that Riley and I decided like three weeks ago, before the team ever qualified for the championship game, that we were going to have a sleepover tonight. I didn't want to cancel."

"Well, I'm sure she'd have understood. You aren't free next weekend?"

"Next weekend is Prom, Mom," I reminded her. "So no. Besides, I want to see her. You know we don't get to hang out much at school anymore. I just texted her, so she should be here any minute."

"Okay. Well, I'm going to sleep in about half an hour, so if you need anything, let me know before then."

"We will."

Mom left for her bedroom and I climbed the stairs to my own. As I changed out of my cheerleading uniform and into a tank top and pajama shorts, I studied myself in the full-length mirror on the back of my bedroom door.

I'd shot up several inches since starting high school, and my awkward middle school phase had long since passed. Back then, I'd have laughed if anyone had told me I'd find high school just as easy to navigate as my older sister had. Evan and Riley were having tougher times, I knew, but it'd seemed so simple to me once I'd figured out how everything worked.

I'd done gymnastics in elementary school, so cheerleading seemed like the best athletic outlet for me. I'd met Vanessa then. And though she was away at college now, back when I'd been a freshman Nicole had taught me how to do my own makeup and had taken me to the mall when I'd asked. And Josh had noticed me my sophomore year. After that, it'd been smooth sailing.

Evan and I didn't really share any classes anymore, because his classes were almost entirely advanced placement. He was also treasurer for the math team. And Riley spent a lot of her spare time at the local skate park with a couple of boys I often saw her in the hallways with. I wondered sometimes if she was into one of them, but if she was, she was lying to me about it.

The three of us weren't exactly distant, and I certainly still felt comfortable around them, but it wasn't the same as it'd been before. Not for me, anyway. I knew between the three of us that I was the weak link: the odd one out. Riley and Evan made time for each other, and to an extent I made time for them too, but I was also busy with Josh and cheerleading.

Thinking about our days at the creek back in middle school made my heart sink, and so I rarely let myself go there. I was well-liked and well-known at school now. I had a boyfriend who was going to be a hero on Monday.

I couldn't have asked for a better high school career.

The front door opened and closed downstairs and I knew it was Riley. One thing hadn't changed in the past few years: Riley never knocked or rang the doorbell. She didn't need to; she was practically family.

She peered around the doorframe and into my room, and then grinned when she saw me. "I watched the game. Come here."

I walked to her, smiling back, and she wrapped me up into a tight hug as she told me, "He was awesome. You could've canceled and I wouldn't have been mad, you know."

"I know." I pulled away to look her in the eyes. "But I wanted to see you. I see Josh all the time."

"He's your boyfriend. I'm your best friend. It's practically my job to be cool with you blowing me off for a guy, right?"

I took in a breath as I studied her, and she stared back, an eyebrow arched like she could tell I felt a little guilty and was judging me for it. She'd dyed a purple streak into the front of her normally auburn hair a month or so ago, and it actually looked really good on her. I'd always thought she was prettier than she gave herself credit for, and I was thinking it again now as I looked at her. I vowed to see how she'd look all dolled up sometime.

"You are, you know," I told her. "My best friend."

"Duh." She pulled away and collapsed onto my bed with a pleased sigh. "Why wouldn't I be? I'm awesome."

"Where's Evan tonight?" I asked, joining her.

12

"Probably asleep. I went to his math competition thing; we got back a couple of hours ago and he was exhausted   ."

"Wait, that was tonight?" I asked, alarmed. "I told him I wanted to come to that."

"Don't worry, I told him it clashed. He understood. The state basketball championship is huge, and besides, you had to go because of cheerleading."

"Yeah, but I still feel bad." I paused. "How did it go?"

"They won, actually. And Evan placed second best overall. Out of like, one hundred people or something. Kid's a genius. I don't know how he does it. The only thing I'm good at is standing on a moving piece of wood."

"Yeah, right. I've seen you take on massive hills without batting an eye. Look at *me*; I just wave pompoms and do cartwheels in a short skirt."

"Oh, no, you do *not* get to have a pity party." She rolled over onto her side to smirk at me. "Let me guess what your plans for next weekend are. You get to go to Prom for free in a dress that makes you look absolutely gorgeous with a guy on your arm that will make every girl in school hate you – other than me, of course – and you're probably riding there in a limo."

"You should come, too. It's not too late," I insisted. "And Evan. Hey! Why don't you guys go together?"

She wrinkled her nose. "No way."

"Just as friends, obviously. Be each other's totally platonic dates for the night. You can wear my sister's old prom dress and borrow shoes from me, and Evan has that tux his mom bought him for his great-aunt's funeral last year. I'll even get you two into our prom group."

"It's way too short notice. Besides, your boyfriend hardly acknowledges our existence."

"Sure he does. He'll let you come along if I ask him to. Think about it? Like, talk to Evan tomorrow and see what he says. I bet he'd go with you."

"Maybe." She shrugged her shoulders. "Where are you guys going after? Any cool parties only the popular kids know about?"

I laughed. "I don't think so. Um. Josh rented a hotel room. I guess he wants—"

"Whoa, no, I know what he wants." She looked taken aback. "He told you he's already rented it?"

"Yeah." I avoided her eyes, suddenly feeling shy.

"Wow. I mean, I knew you guys hadn't... but it's kind of blatant, isn't it?"

"Well, he's graduating in two months."

"But didn't he get a basketball scholarship to some big school in Cali?"

"Yeah."

"So how does that work?"

I sighed and shrugged my shoulders. "We don't really talk about it."

"Sooo... he wants to take you to Prom, have sex with you, and then...? No plans after that? He's just going to school really far away and isn't talking about how that's gonna affect the two of you?" She looked dubious.

"Well, I think it's just hard to talk about. He's probably sad that we'll be so far apart."

"Still, it's maybe something you should have a

conversation about before he leaves. What if he's—" She cut herself off, hesitating.

"What?" I pressed. Her tone told me she thought taking Josh up on his offer was a bad idea. Truthfully, I'd been wondering myself if it was the right time. I liked Josh, but we still hadn't worked out what we were going to do after his graduation.

Riley took in a sharp breath. "Okay. I'm not trying to— I'm just trying to be a good friend. Maybe I'm totally off base; I don't really know the guy. But... just make sure he's serious about doing the long-distance thing before you have sex with him. I mean, right? If he already knows it's not gonna work out after he graduates, then he'd be kind of an ass to do the whole hotel room thing after Prom. And it's weird that he won't even talk about it."

"No, you're right." I bit at my lip and stared at the ceiling, acutely aware of Riley still watching me on my left. "I mean... do you think I shouldn't go to the room? Maybe I could just tell him to take me home after the dance."

I turned to face her, and her eyes snapped down to where her hand had begun to pick at my comforter. "I think you should do what you want to do," she said. "Just be careful, is all. I don't want to see you get your heart broken."

I studied her for a moment, and then gave her a small smile. Evan was smarter than Riley and me, but she always gave the best advice. "You're always looking out for me. And I pretty much never get to return the favor because you never put yourself in a position to screw up."

"Yeah. I know." She looked up at me, grinning smugly, and I shoved her onto her back and then pinned her arms with one hand, using my free one to jab her in the ribs. She shouted at me through her laughter, "No! Your freaking cheerleading muscles!" and when she finally managed to wriggle her way out of my grip, she retaliated by punching me in the shoulder.

"Ow!" I rubbed at the throbbing spot as she sat up and twisted around to face me. Then I pouted up at her. "Take Evan to prom so I don't feel bad about going alone?"

"Yes, you will be *so* alone. With your cheerleading friends and their boyfriends and *your* boyfr—"

"You know what I mean," I interrupted. "I want to go with my best friends. You guys loved me even when I was twelve and lanky and awkward." I grabbed at her hand, clasping it between mine, and raised it to my chest. "Pleeeease?"

She heaved a sigh and rolled her eyes, something that Riley did a lot. Mostly because both Evan and I constantly gave her reason to. *"Okay.* I'll ask him. And by that, I mean I'll force him to come with me. But you better get us into that limo, because, as you know, Evan's car is a literal pile of metal garbage and he's also a terrible driver. If I have to ride with him, you'll be coming to my funeral instead of Josh's graduation in a couple of months."

I beamed at her and tackled her into a hug. "Thank

you!"

***

Josh was still on a high after the game on Monday. Everywhere he went, the students who'd seen it congratulated him, and the few who hadn't watched it quickly made sure that they were filled in.

As per usual, I joined him and a few of his friends at lunch, along with Vanessa, and nudged him midway through a conversation about a new video game that'd come out over the weekend. "Hey, can I talk to you about something?"

"Hmm?" He twisted to face me, confused for a moment, like he'd only half heard me. "Oh, yeah. What's up?"

"It's about our Prom group. Do we have room for a couple more people in the limo?"

He exchanged a look with the boy across the table from him—Sean, his burly football player of a best friend—and then smirked. "Depends on who you're asking for."

"Not funny," I replied, though I smacked his arm lightly to let him know I wasn't actually angry. "My other friends might come along."

He took a bite of a biscuit and then spoke with his mouth full, looking confused. "What other friends?"

"You know..." I shifted uncomfortably when he still seemed genuinely confused. He didn't know who I was talking about. "I've told you about them. I hung out with

17

them when I was a kid."

"Oh, you mean the math gee- uh, guy, and the chick with the purple hair?"

I suppressed an eye-roll at his slip up, and told him, "Riley's hair isn't purple, it's like one streak, and yes, I want her and Evan to come with us."

"Why?"

"Because they're my *friends*."

"No, I know, but don't they have their own group?"

"They weren't gonna go at all. I'm trying to talk them into coming."

"Why?" he asked again, and I heaved a sigh.

"Look, if you don't want them to come with us, you can just say so."

"Hey, whoa." He reached out to rub at my back. "Chill out, Kayla. If you want them there, then they can be there. I was just asking. For thirty bucks each, they're in, and I'll pick them both up at your house when I come to get you. Sound good?"

"Yeah," I replied shortly, still a little sour. I'd never spent more than a minute with Josh, Riley, and Evan all at the same time, but it still hurt that he hadn't remembered they existed. "Perfect."

***

"I can't believe I let you talk me into doing this."

"Gasp! Conformity!" I mocked Riley, motioning for her to spin around on the stool in my bathroom. "You're gonna lose all your street cred."

18

"Don't ever use that phrase. You can't pull it off, cheerleader."

"What are your guys doing tonight, anyway? I'm guessing they're not going?"

"Oh, Dylan and Brett? Yeah, there's actually this skate event happening tonight at the park. It's a competition for two hundred bucks, I think, but you have to be able to land a kickflip to even compete, and kickflips, naturally, happen to be my kryptonite. Just my luck."

"Kickflips. Right. Those things I am totally familiar with." I looked away from her to reach for an eyeliner pencil, but didn't miss her eye-roll. "Okay, sit really, *really* still."

"Don't you have to do this for yourself, too? You don't have to do mine. I'll just go like this."

"We have three hours, Riley. I'm sure I'll be fine."

She heaved another sigh but obeyed my instructions, and I leaned in close to get a better look as I ran the pencil first along her lower lashes, and then her upper ones. I pulled away and grinned. "Oh, wow." She started to turn back around to face the mirror, and I stopped her. "Wait until I'm totally done. It'll be a bigger shock that way."

"Fine." She fell silent as I added eyeshadow and then mascara, and as I reached for foundation, she asked, "So how much does your boyfriend hate you for making him bring us along?"

"It wasn't hard to get you guys in, actually," I told her. "I keep telling you he isn't as much of an ass as you think he is if you really get to know him. He's actually really sweet."

"Well, of course he's sweet to *you*." She paused. "I forgot to tell you he called me 'Barney' last week because of my hair. I don't think he remembered who I was; you've only introduced us once."

I was taken aback. That didn't sound like the Josh I knew. "Are you serious?"

"Scout's honor. But I'm sure he's great to the girl he's dating. I mean, maybe that's what's important?"

I was too perturbed to pretend to agree, and shook my head to myself as I covered Riley's face with foundation. Next, I reached for blush and applied it to the apples of her cheeks. "Him respecting my friends is what's important to me." I pulled away to admire my handiwork, and my eyes widened, Josh momentarily forgotten. "Whoa."

"What?" She pressed a hand to her cheek, self-conscious. "Does it look bad? I knew I shouldn't have-"

"No, Riley, stop. Holy crap, you're beautiful." And she was. My compliment came out stronger than I'd intended, and I added, "Evan is gonna love it," to ease the strange tension that'd filled our small room.

It worked. She swatted at my stomach and replied, "Shut up!" while I smirked at her.

"Look," I demanded, and motioned for her to spin around. She faced herself in the mirror and raised both eyebrows, clearly surprised, but not quite as surprised as I'd been.

"Wow. I'm... kinda hot?"

"Kind of? You're totally worthy of a first-stringer. Vanessa's going to Prom with the backup quarterback, you know."

"Ah, yes, just the kind of guy I want. A jock. Don't project your awful taste onto me."

"Oh, yeah?" I countered, putting both of my hands on her shoulders and leaning into her so that my cheek was pressed to hers. Together, we stared into the mirror as I asked her, "What's your type, then? Skaters?" She rolled her eyes and I studied her for a moment, then shook my head. "No, too obvious. What about guys with tattoos? Future English majors who write poetry?" I lit up, feigning a gasp of realization. "Redheads!"

She didn't laugh. Instead, she just watched the two of us for a moment, and I saw her swallow hard as she shrugged me off of her shoulder. I knew before she answered that she wasn't going to tell me. "I don't know."

"How can you not know?" It seemed so easy to me. Once I'd seen enough boys I'd found attractive, it hadn't been hard to find a pattern. "You know, I always thought the one thing our friendship needed was more guy talk. You never *ever* talk about who you like. It's always just been me talking and you listening." I reached for a tube of lip-gloss as I told her, "So you talk, and I'll listen. There must be someone you kind of deep down wanted to go to Prom with. Open your mouth." When she shot me a weird look, I elaborated, "I mean for the lip gloss."

"How am I supposed to talk and also let you put that stuff on me?" she asked, gesturing to the tube in my hand.

"This first. Boys after," I replied simply, reaching out for her chin to steady her. She went eerily silent, then, and my gaze fell to her lips as I concentrated on spreading the gloss along her top lip. "When I'm done with this," I told her gently, "just rub your lips together. If it still feels like too much, we can dab at it until it doesn't."

I finished with her top lip and moved to the bottom one, my hand still on her chin. She had a fuller bottom lip than Josh, I noticed, and then wondered why on earth that'd crossed my mind. Maybe because this was the closest I'd been to anyone's lips besides Josh's lately. And the closest I'd ever been to Riley's.

I pulled away with a strange twinge in my chest, and shook it off with a dramatic, "Ta-da!"

Riley looked a little out of it for a moment, like she had her mind elsewhere, and now she cleared her throat and gave me a smile I knew well enough to realize was forced. "Thanks."

I arched an eyebrow, surprised she was even trying to act enthused at all. "Thanks? Are you actually starting to appreciate my effort?"

She blinked a couple of times, still distracted, and then finally managed a snappy retort. "I was just caught off-guard by my own hotness. Slight lapse in brain function."

"Hmm." I studied her for a moment, pleased to see she seemed to being growing self-conscious under my gaze.

"What?"

"I'm trying to decide what to do with your hair."

"Oh, jeez," she sighed out.

"I'm curling it," I declared. "And while I do it, you're going to tell me what your type is." She groaned as I plugged the curling iron in and grabbed a brush to get the tangles out of her hair. "Go!"

"Alright, alright. I like... greasy hair. And yellow teeth; really poor hygiene is a must. The stronger the stench, the better."

"I'm serious!" I gathered her hair in one hand and tugged a little. "Don't lie to me; I'm holding your hair hostage."

"Take it all but leave my purple streak! I don't care! You'll never get it out of me!"

"You suck," I shot back, and began to brush her hair out. "You know what? Just date Evan. I'm going to assume that's your type until you tell me."

"You are literally the worst. Why do I still hang out with you?"

"Because I'm adorable." I set the brush aside and combed my fingers through her hair affectionately while I waited for the curling iron to heat up.

She watched me in the mirror for a long moment, and then said, at last, "Brunettes."

I stared back at her, surprised. "Hmm?"

"You wanted to know something about my type. I like dark hair." She played with the hem of her shirt: a nervous habit of hers. "Evan's blond, so."

"But he has a great personality," I pointed out, kidding.

"You would seriously want me to date Evan?"

23

"I'm definitely just messing with you. I mean, unless it was what *you* wanted…"

She rolled her eyes but didn't reply. I wondered for a moment if she was just trying to throw me off with the whole brunette thing. Maybe she really did like Evan and was just embarrassed about it. I hadn't forgotten about how he'd crushed on her when we were kids, and my opinion on Evan pairing off with either of us hadn't changed. We were three, not a two and a one.

I curled Riley's hair with, thankfully, little complaint from her, creating loose ringlets that framed her face, and when I was finished, we had two hours to go until Josh's arrival. "Done," I announced, and unplugged the curling iron while Riley studied herself in the mirror.

"You really think I look good?"

"You're prettier than me," I told her, meaning it.

"It doesn't have to be a competition," she replied with a frown.

"You're right." I leaned into her from behind, squeezing her shoulders, and carefully kissed her on the top of her head. "But it were, you'd win." I let her go without waiting for a response, and left the bathroom to go grab the dresses we'd be wearing. "My turn!" I called back, and heard her slip off of the stool and pad across the bathroom floor.

"This night will never end," she groaned.

"We can only hope!" I replied.

***

Evan rang the doorbell downstairs just as Riley and I were finishing getting dressed. I adjusted my ocean blue dress as beside me, Riley struggled with Nicole's old one. The dark green looked good on her, but she was obviously having some sort of moral dilemma over it as she twisted and turned in the mirror. "Are you sure I look okay?" she asked me.

"Yes!" I said. "You really do look great."

"What if I get there and people laugh? What if they think it's sad that I'd even try? I mean, this is so clearly not anything I'd ever voluntarily wear, and people pick up on that kind of stuff, you know? I'm going to radiate insecurity."

"The only strange looks you're going to get will be from people who are amazed that they never realized how attractive you are," I assured her. "You're that girl in the movies that shows up to Prom and everyone wonders who she is and why they'd never noticed her before."

"I hate that girl," Riley mumbled. "Make-up doesn't make girls beautiful. Confidence makes girls beautiful, and in case you haven't noticed, I am lacking that tonight."

"You'll be fine. Trust me," I said, and reached out to grip both of her hands in mine. "You're just stepping out of your comfort zone. If you put me in a helmet and elbow pads and made me try to ride a skateboard I'd probably freak out too, so I get it. But if you looked like an ogre, I'd tell you. If someone gets to slow dance with you tonight, he... or *she* will be a very lucky person."

"She?" Riley echoed, alarmed.

I snickered at the look on her face. "Relax, it was a joke. You know, because you're pretty enough to turn a few girls gay for the night?" I nudged her as I moved past her to the door. "Keep up. We should go keep Evan company; it sounds like he's waiting downstairs."

"Okay," she replied very quietly, and a moment later, I heard her following me.

Evan's eyes widened to the size of saucers when he saw me, and then, if possible, they grew even wider when Riley appeared. "Whoa! Riley! And Kayla, you too, duh, but... Riley!"

"I understand," I told him, and reached up to ruffle his hair a little. "Go messier; it suits you. You look nice."

"Thanks." He grinned at me as I looked him up and down. He'd grown to be a good head taller than Riley and me, and he was wearing a pretty standard black tuxedo with a black bowtie, white undershirt, and black shoes. He was handsome in a way only Evan tended to be. He was a little awkward and a little geeky, but endearing all the same. "You guys are totally outshining me, though. How did you make Riley into a girl?"

He laughed at his own joke, and I turned to see Riley with her middle finger in the air as she shot a glare his way. "I'm still man enough to kick your ass, Faulkner."

"Okay," I cut in, motioning for them to settle down. "Try not to kill each other before we even get to the dance."

"Oh, you guys!"

That was Mom, entering with her phone gripped in one hand. She raised it and snapped a photo without warning us, and I winced as the flash temporarily left spots on my vision.

"Ouch, Mom, give us a heads up next time."

"I need a picture to send to your sister; she wanted to see," Mom said. "Riley, I hardly recognize you! Nicole is going to love you in her dress."

"Thanks, Ms. Copeland," Riley replied, tight-lipped.

"So when's Josh getting here again?" Evan asked me. "You said it'd be half an hour when I was on my way. I'm ready to get this thing over with."

"You too?" I sighed. "C'mon, Prom is supposed to be fun!"

"Yeah, but *Zombie Guts 3* came out last weekend and Riley owes me a round. We're playing it at my house after the dance." He glanced toward my mom and added, hastily, "As you know, since you're coming too and we're forcing you to watch."

I shot him a thankful look as Mom snapped another picture of us. "Let me go get your boutonnieres, girls," she said, and left for her bedroom.

"Oh, that reminds me. Here," said Evan, offering Riley the corsage in his hand. She slid it onto her wrist distractedly, watching me.

"I thought you hadn't decided on the whole hotel thing yet?"

I shrugged my shoulders. "I haven't. All I know at this point is that our entire group is leaving the dance at the same time – eleven o'clock – and the limo is taking us back to Josh's place. Then he'll drive us back here to drop you guys off, and... either I'll get out of the car too or I won't."

"Seems like it'd be easy for that to go badly," Evan said.

"Maybe." I shrugged my shoulders, fidgeting with one of the straps of my dress. "But at least if I back out, I'll be home and I can just walk to Evan's with you guys. And anyway, it's not like it's an ultimatum, right? I mean, he didn't make it seem like one. He wouldn't break up with me just because I said no to a night in a hotel room."

"If you say so," replied Evan, shrugging back.

Riley was oddly silent on my other side, and I turned to her to ask, "What do you think?"

She shrugged, too. "Like I said: you should do what you want."

"Well, I know he's not you guys' favorite person, but he's a better guy than you give him credit for. You'll see tonight," I assured them.

Mom returned with our boutonnieres, and Riley examined hers for a moment, confused. "Wait, how does this work?"

"I'll show you when Josh gets here," I started to say, but the doorbell rang and I lit up. "Good timing!" I went to the door and opened it.

It was Josh, as I'd expected. He offered himself up, arms stretched out to the sides, and asked me, "How do I look?"

His tuxedo was sky blue with a matching tie, and he'd put hair gel into his black hair to make it lay flatter. He looked older than he usually did. "Very handsome," I told him as I took his hand to lead him inside. "I was just telling Riley she needs to watch me pin this thing on you."

"Hi, Josh," Riley very clearly forced herself to say, and Evan good-naturedly offered his hand for Josh to shake.

"Hey, guys," Josh replied, and then did a double-take as he looked to Riley. "Wait… purple hair girl?"

"The one and only," Riley replied. I could practically see her resisting the urge to roll her eyes and held back a sigh myself.

"Nice!" Josh looked to Evan and told him, "You're a lucky dude," which very quickly caused Evan's face to heat up.

"No, ah… well, thanks, but we're friendly. Friends. Just going as friends, I mean."

"Oh. Whoops."

"Here, you just stick it on the lapel like this," I told Riley, hastily redirecting the conversation. She watched me, then walked to Evan and mimicked my actions. Hers was a little crooked, but Evan straightened it once she'd stepped away.

Josh slipped his corsage onto my wrist and then offered me his arm. "Shall we go?"

"Not without pictures!" Mom interrupted. I'd almost forgotten she was there.

"Oh, sure thing, Ms. Copeland," Josh agreed. She took a few pictures of just Josh and I, some of just Evan and Riley, and then a few of the three of us, without Josh. When we all got together for a group picture, it was with Riley and me in the center. I reached out and took her hand.

"Say cheese and smile!" Mom called out. "One, two, three..."

Riley's hand squeezed mine tighter, and I grinned as the camera flashed.

Chapter Two

It was strange to me that Evan kept an arm wrapped around Riley throughout the drive to the dance.

I noticed it first when we were five minutes into our limo ride, and the two of them were sitting across from Josh and me. Vanessa was on my other side, and I half-listened to her go on about the songs she hoped the DJ would play, my eyes fixed, unmoving, on the way Riley leaned on Evan and his hand rested against the seat on her opposite side, his arm stretched out behind her back. It seemed oddly possessive, and while I knew they were both wary of their company and clinging to each other for support, I didn't like the look of them together the way they were.

Then I began to wonder if I'd made a mistake asking them to come with me together. Evan had liked Riley for years, and I'd just assumed his crush had faded because it was no longer obvious. But what if he'd just gotten better at hiding it? And what if Riley was lying and felt the same way? Was I just a side character in some kind of epic love story they'd both be telling their grandchildren in sixty years?

The thought made me shudder, and that caught Josh's attention. "Cold?" he asked me.

"I'm fine," I insisted, and resumed pretending to listen to Vanessa. I glanced to Riley again and caught her eye, and she offered me a small smile.

I forced one back, picturing an elderly Riley and Evan describing how they'd met in first grade and always kind of liked each other and just never had the guts to act on it until this *other* friend of theirs – because in my horrific vision, I was no longer around and was left nameless – had made them go to their junior Prom together, where they'd finally gathered the courage to admit how they felt.

I shuddered again, feeling as though I'd potentially made a terrible mistake. Neither of them had even wanted to go in the first place. Maybe I shouldn't have pushed.

Our group stopped for dinner, where I mostly ate in silence, too busy disturbing myself with the idea of Evan and Riley together to hold a conversation. We showed up at the dance another hour later, and Josh immediately pulled me out onto the dance floor.

I forced myself to cheer up. I was probably just paranoid. Riley had never shown an interest in dating, and there was no reason to believe she'd start now.

Still, I kept an eye on the two of them on and off over the course of the night. They mostly stuck together, dancing to the fast songs with each other and awkwardly agreeing to leave the floor for the slow songs. I abandoned Josh, Vanessa, and the others to dance with the two of them a couple of times, which, unsurprisingly, were the more fun dances of the night.

As the dance wound down and the fast songs gave way to slower ones, I stayed pressed to Josh, my hands hooked behind his neck while his rested on my back and waist.

"I'm so ready for tonight," he murmured into my neck, and I inhaled deeply and closed my eyes. I wasn't sure that I was ready, but I wanted to be.

I pulled away from him a little and looked around. Vanessa was pressed close to her date, and they were making out, which had already gotten them into trouble twice already. I chuckled a little and shook my head, then searched the crowd around us for Evan and Riley. I couldn't find them on the edge of the dance floor.

When I checked my other side, I realized why. They were a few feet away, swaying together with a gap between them. It was very middle school. I caught Riley's eye and she gave me a small shrug, as if to say, "Yeah, I don't know, either," and it made me laugh again. I knew for sure I'd been paranoid, then. It didn't matter that they were slow-dancing together. Riley didn't like Evan. Riley didn't like anyone. She was just above the whole high school dating thing, I supposed.

And maybe that was the best way to be. Here I was, with a dark cloud hanging over my head and a half-hearted commitment to sharing a hotel room with a boy I wasn't sure even *wanted* to do the long-distance thing. I liked Josh, but it'd certainly been stressful to be with him this year.

Eleven o'clock came, and those of us in our Prom group who hadn't already found an alternative way to leave the dance early piled into the limo. I sat between Josh and Riley this time, exhausted, and felt her lips press to my ear. When she spoke, her breath tickled, creating goosebumps on my arms. "Do you know what you're doing yet?"

I shook my head silently, and she sat back, visibly disappointed. A part of me knew that for all her efforts to be a supportive, impartial best friend, she very clearly didn't want me to go with Josh. Probably because she didn't *like* Josh. But they were from two different worlds, so it was understandable. It didn't mean either of them were bad people.

When we reached Josh's home, I said goodbye to Vanessa and got into his car with Riley and Evan. I fidgeted all the way to my house, very aware of Riley and Evan staring holes in my cheek and the back of my head from the seats behind Josh and me. Josh reached over with his free hand and took hold of mine. I breathed in slowly as we pulled up in front of my house, suddenly feeling very hot, and rolled my window down to get some cool air on my face.

"Good times, you guys," Josh told Riley and Evan

distractedly, examining his hair in his rear-view mirror. I nudged him, and he turned around to smile at them. "Seriously. It was fun. Riley, you looked really pretty tonight; I'm impressed."

"Thanks," Riley replied flatly. She got out of the car on my side while Evan exited on Josh's side, and I hesitated, glancing to Josh, who had gone back to checking himself out in the mirror. I didn't know what to do.

Riley paused outside of my window and arched an eyebrow at me in a silent question.

"Um." I shot her a desperate look, hoping she wouldn't be upset, and then said, "I'll see you tomorrow?"

She stood there for a moment that felt much longer than it was. And then her gaze dropped to the ground, and she shrugged her shoulders and moved away from the car. "Yeah, whatever."

I let out a sigh and pressed the back of my head to the seat, inwardly berating myself for getting stuck in between my boyfriend and my best friends in the first place. Josh started his car back up again, and we drove away.

***

The hotel room was nicer than I'd expected it to be. There was a mini-fridge, a television, a bed much bigger than the one I slept in at home, and even a couple of complementary bottles of water.

"Sweet," said Josh when he spotted the water. "I

35

didn't know they gave us that."

"Free water, imagine that," I joked. He rounded on me, grinning, and then hoisted me into the air and carried me to the bed. I laughed the whole way despite myself; he'd always had a way of making me feel comfortable when I was second-guessing something. It was one of the things I liked most about him.

We kissed for a moment with him hovering over me, before I lay back on the bed and swallowed hard. "I've never..." I started to say, and his smile faded.

"I know." He hesitated, and then admitted, "I actually haven't either."

I was taken aback. He had so much more dating experience than I did. "But-"

"But I'm the basketball captain? But I've had other girlfriends?" He shrugged. "You and I started dating when I was sixteen. I never actually got around to it before then, and when we started talking, I thought it'd be cool if it were you. Because I really liked you." He brushed a strand of my hair away from my face. "So... here we are."

I swallowed hard and reached up to touch his cheek. I didn't want to ruin our night, but I agreed with Riley that I had to get the elephant in the room taken care of before we went any further. "But what about after this?"

He sighed and hung his head for a moment, and then shot me an exasperated look. I knew then that he'd been hoping to avoid this discussion. "Why do we have to worry about that right now? We'll figure it out later."

"You always say that," I insisted, sitting up. "You

36

always say we'll figure it out later. But this is a big deal to me, and I don't want to have this moment with a guy who doesn't see a future with me. Even if I am only seventeen."

"But in this moment, right now, it isn't about the future. It's about me and you, and the fact that we've been planning this for months now. We said Prom night at the latest, and c'mon, Kayla, it's Prom night! Life is too short to not live in the now, so just..." He leaned in and I pressed a hand to his chest, stopping him. He sighed and climbed off of me, running a hand through his hair.

"I want to have this conversation tonight," I told him.

"Why tonight? Literally every night other than tonight would be better than tonight!"

"Then we should've had it before now," I countered. "But we didn't because you wouldn't, so here we are. What happens after graduation?"

He shrugged his shoulders. "How am I supposed to know? All I know is that I'll be in California, and you'll be here. And it's, like, a ten-hour drive or something, so... I guess it's gonna be kind of hard to visit."

"And there'll be a ton of girls there," I reminded him. "Really attractive girls from California."

"C'mon, Kayla, it's not like I don't think you're attractive. I never shut up about how hot I think you are."

"Well, you might feel a little differently when you haven't seen me in two months and a girl a year older than you is walking to the communal dorm bathroom in just a towel," I retorted, rolling my eyes.

"What, you think I'm just gonna sleep with the first girl that pays attention to me? That's really what you think of me?"

"No, I just think that you'll probably meet someone and... what if something happens, and then I'm here alone? Or... what if I find someone else here when you're not around?"

At that, he tensed, and I fell silent, biting anxiously at my lip. He shook his head.

"If you wanna date someone else, you should just say it."

"I don't!" I groaned and pressed a hand to my forehead, squeezing my eyes shut. "But how are we supposed to date someone we never see?"

Josh was silent for a while, his legs crossed in front of him and his chin in his hands. At last, he said, "Maybe we aren't."

I looked over at him, letting out a deep sigh. He'd come to the same conclusion that I had, deep down, several weeks ago. It was only now that I was finally acknowledging that conclusion. "You really think so?"

"I don't know. It kind of seems like long-distance relationships don't work out. Do you even want to go to school in California?"

"It'd be nice. But I won't have the scholarships that you do, and my mom didn't have the money to send my sister anywhere out of state, so I'll probably have to stay in-state, too. So... we'd be living in different states until you graduate. In-" I inhaled deeply, pausing. "In four years."

There was a long silence, and then Josh mumbled, "So that's it? We're really just gonna call it quits on Prom night?"

"You're not leaving yet," I reminded him half-heartedly. "There's still the next two months, and then summer."

"But you don't want to do tonight, so why would you want to keep dating me?"

I hesitated, and then admitted, "I wouldn't. I kind of just said it because I didn't know what else to say."

"I figured." He looked over at me, sighed, and then leaned over to kiss me on the cheek. "You sure you don't want to have sex tonight?" he joked.

"Pretty sure."

He stood and offered me his hand, then helped me get to my feet. "Figured it was worth a shot. It'd be nice to have a good final memory to look back on, you know? You're... you, uh, *were* my first real girlfriend." He winced, and gave his head a quick shake, reaching up to pinch the bridge of his nose. His voice choked up, he mumbled, "Shit."

I stood on my toes and pulled him close for a long kiss, and then told him, trying to keep my own voice steady, "I'll miss you." Maybe it *had* been inevitable, but that didn't make it any easier.

He pressed his forehead to mine and I felt his hands tremble at my waist. "Well, I miss you already," he said.

***

It was after midnight when I finally got back home, so I resisted the urge to text Evan and Riley and waited until morning. I knew that Vanessa was probably the better person to go to and that Evan and Riley had never really liked Josh, but they were also my best friends, and I wanted my best friends to be the ones to get me through my first major break-up.

I cried a lot that night. I'd been with Josh for a year and a half, and I wasn't going to just immediately be over it, even despite the fact that I'd sort of initiated our break-up. I didn't know how to handle it. Could I still talk to him, or was that not allowed? Could I even text him? Would he even want me to?

I woke up feeling groggy the next morning, and after I showered and changed, I picked up my phone to contact Evan and Riley. My eyebrows furrowed when I saw I had a text message from Evan already. It said exactly what I'd wanted to send him: "*Creek?*"

"*Ten minutes,*" I sent back, and went downstairs to tell my mom where I was going. She tried to ask me questions about Prom, but I avoided them. The longer I could go without mentioning breaking up with Josh to her, the better. I didn't want to deal with her meltdown when I was still trying to prevent having one of my own.

I didn't text Riley, mostly because I assumed that Evan had texted her to come to the creek, too. So I was surprised to see Evan alone at our old makeshift shelter when I got there.

His eyes were closed, and he looked completely

drained. He didn't even look my way until I was standing right next to him. "Rough night?" I joked.

"I could ask you the same thing," he fired back.

"Ha ha. Where's Riley?"

"Left her out of this one. She's not answering my texts, anyway." He sighed deeply and elaborated, before I could even ask, "I think I screwed up last night."

I sat down next to him, concerned. He still wouldn't meet my eyes. "Oh, god, Evan, what did you do? Did you guys have a fight?"

"I kissed her," he groaned, looking to me at last.

My eyes widened. I was sure I'd misheard him. "*What?*"

"I kissed Riley. After the dance we went to my house to play video games and we were hanging out and talking and she looked pretty and you *know* – don't act like you don't – that I've always kind of liked her and I just kind of kissed her."

"Okay." I tried hard to absorb every word with a straight face. "So she pushed you away and then what?"

"Pushed me away?" he asked, confused. "What? No, we made out for like... I don't know, a few minutes? Maybe even close to ten or fifteen. It felt like a long time."

I went through a range of emotions in that moment, and, frankly, deserved an Oscar for keeping my face from changing. First, there was alarm, for obvious reasons. Then, also obviously, disgust. But then there was a third emotion I couldn't identify, though it felt like a searing heat that started in my stomach, shot to my heart (it stayed there, burning, for a few seconds), and then exited through my ears like invisible steam. But it wasn't entirely like anger.

"You made out with Riley," I echoed dumbly. "Riley made out with you."

"Yeah. I mean, I knew I wasn't imagining things," he said. "There was always something there, you know? And we made out for a while, which was... *really* nice-"

"Okay, I got that part," I interrupted.

"And then she kind of... freaked out and left."

The searing feeling faded slightly. That sounded more like Riley. "Freaked out how?"

"Well, we were kissing, and then we stopped kissing, and she didn't push me away or anything but we just sort of stopped and kind of just sat together for a few seconds. Then she said she had to go, practically ran out, and isn't returning my calls or texts. And I'm guessing you haven't talked to her because you look totally freaked out right now." He said all of this in one breath, with very few pauses, and I blinked a couple of times, trying to keep up.

"Yeah," I said at last, my throat feeling a little tighter than usual. It showed in my voice. "Totally freaked."

"I know it's weird. For you, I mean; for me it's kind of something that only happened in my dreams, but-"

"Please, no more," I said weakly, waving my hand at him. "No dreams. No more details."

"Okay." He took a deep breath. "I can do that."

I stared at him, feeling sick. "... *fifteen minutes*?"

"Yeah," he breathed out, going somewhere else in his head for a moment. I punched his knee, hard, and he yelped. "Ow!"

"Why!?" I cried out. "Why would you do this to me? It was the three of us, Evan! The Three Musketeers! The three amigos! The three... freaking Powerpuff Girls; I don't know! Bubbles and Buttercup didn't start dating!"

"Well, they were sisters, and also six years old," he input quietly, and then, louder, added, "Wait, am I Bubbles?"

"Yes!" I snapped.

He frowned, offended. "Look, anyway, I asked you here because I wanted you to help me fix this."

"Done," I agreed. I was already on top of it. "I'll go to Riley, let her know you're cool with being just friends, and then hopefully you won't have ruined our trio and we can put this all behind us and-"

"Wait, no," he interrupted. "None of that, Kayla. Didn't you hear me say that I've had a crush on Riley for years? Or that she kissed me back?"

"I think I repressed all of that about ten seconds ago, actually, but thanks for reminding me."

"I need you to talk to her for me and find out if she has feelings for me like I do for her," Evan pressed. "Or if maybe she thinks that she could. Or even if she just thought she did last night. I know it's weird because it's Riley and me, but, I mean... this is the girl of my dreams. She's everything to me. And you're right, I want to preserve our friendship if that's what it comes to, but if there's even a chance that she could like me back, you have to encourage her, *please*." He clasped his hands together and widened his eyes, silently begging me. I felt

43

sick to my stomach again.

"God. This is... the worst past twelve hours of my life," I decided. "Yes. I'll do it." How could I not? I'd be the worst friend ever if I refused.

"Thank you," he sighed, and wrapped me up in a tight hug. I pressed my face into his shoulder, trying to hold back a sob, and very quickly failing. Seconds later, I was soaking his shirt and he was squeaking my name like he wasn't sure how to react. "I didn't realize- uh... Kayla?"

"Josh and I broke up last night," I sobbed into his neck, and Evan relaxed and rubbed at my back.

"Oh, man. That's terrible. I thought you guys were gonna...? And so did Riley."

"We were." I pulled away from him and sniffed, wiping at my eyes. "But he's leaving for college, and I told him I didn't want to have sex if we were going to break up anyway, and so we kind of broke up now rather than later." I shook my head, gesturing toward him. "And then I wake up to *this*!"

Evan winced and I moved to sit beside him, then let him wrap an arm around me and pull me close. We sat in silence for some time while I tried, with Evan's help, to calm myself down. "Riley was real upset at first last night," Evan finally told me. "After you left. She couldn't even get into killing zombies, so I turned it off and we talked for a little while."

"She was that upset that I didn't come hang out with you guys?" I asked him. "Why? She doesn't like Josh, but he was always a good boyfriend."

"I don't know, I guess she just really didn't like him.

That's all she said, anyway. We kinda stopped talking after that."

"Why, what-" I wrinkled my nose. "Ugh! Okay, right."

"Yeah..."

I let out a heavy sigh, and then leaned my head on his shoulder. "I'll talk to her," I vowed, and in my head, added, *"but I'm not gonna like it."*

Chapter Three

Once it sank in that quite possibly my literal worst nightmare had come true, I took an hour to myself in my bedroom to gather my bearings. Riley wasn't answering my only text to her, which had asked her if I could come over and talk, so she was probably upset. At me for leaving last night or Evan for kissing her or at both of us for the combination of the two, I wasn't sure.

Regardless, now that I was stuck in the middle of my literal worst nightmare, I needed a plan of action.

Firstly, I had to recognize that my literal worst nightmare was probably not Riley's literal worst nightmare, and that it was Evan's literal dream come true, so I couldn't screw it up for them, as much as I would've liked to. My job was to be a good best friend, even if that meant proverbially stabbing myself several times in the chest and stomach area with a talking sword that repeatedly shouted "You are the weakest link, goodbye!" while Riley and Evan skipped off into the sunset with their traitorous hands traitorously linked between them.

"Ugh," I mumbled aloud at the mental image.

Secondly, in order to be at my optimal best-friendliness, I had to put aside my break-up with Josh. If I shoved the sad feelings down long enough, they'd probably just go away eventually. That sounded healthy and totally correct.

At the moment, my focus had to be on the needs of my best friends. Both Riley and Evan, as far as I knew, had never kissed anyone before last night – other than that unfortunate Spin the Bottle incident with Evan and me at age twelve – and so they were both having new and scary experiences, *and* they'd lost one of the two people they had available to talk to about those experiences. Only I remained.

Thirdly... I had to be able to hold back my puke.

"You've got this." I stared at myself in my bedroom mirror, teeth gritted. "You have no emotions. You are a robot. No more tears. No more nausea. No more of that weird chest feeling. It's all gonna be just *fine*. They're definitely not third-wheeling you." I stood still, breathing hard, then bit back a sob and turned to hastily leave my room.

If Riley wouldn't come to me, I'd have to go to Riley.

***

The good thing about living in the same neighborhood as my two best friends was that it was easy to go see each other when we wanted to.

The bad thing about living in the same neighborhood was that, well, it was easy to go see each other when one of us *didn't* want to.

Normally, this meant that if any of us were fighting, it was an easy fix. Someone just had to crack first and show up at the others' houses.

Riley'd outsmarted at me. When I knocked on her front door, her mom answered and told me she was off somewhere in the neighborhood on her skateboard. Given that my house and Evan's were both down the road in one direction and she was clearly avoiding both of us, it was obvious she'd probably headed in the other. I started walking.

I thought about what I'd say to Riley when I saw her. I thought about how well I'd be able to bite my tongue and avoid saying what I really thought. I wanted to beg her not to do this to our group.

Riley dating Evan meant that there was a chance they'd eventually break up, so even if I managed to get past feeling left out while they were dating, I'd eventually have to deal with the fallout of the end of their relationship. I didn't want to lose either of them.

But I also didn't want to be selfish. I'd dated a few guys already, and they'd both listened to all my stories and complaints and saw me through the break-ups. I knew Evan and Riley both deserved a turn now. I just wished it wasn't with *each other*.

I must've walked for at least ten minutes before I finally heard the sound of wheels on gravel. I looked up and saw Riley headed down the street toward me, decked out in knee and elbow pads and wearing her trademark Converses. All traces of how I'd altered her appearance last night were gone.

I stopped and waited for her to reach me, and she pushed off harder as she came closer, like she was trying to pick up speed. "Riley," I tried, and she blew right past me.

"Busy," she told me shortly, and then she was riding away at a runner's pace. I sighed and looked down at my shoes. Flats. They'd have to do.

"Wait up!"

I took off after Riley, sprinting until my chest hurt. She stayed at a constant speed, just a few feet in front of me.

"Riley, c'mon! What did I do?"

She turned around briefly to shoot me a strange look. "Nothing. I just need to practice."

I rolled my eyes and slowed down, entirely aware that she was full of it. I watched her head down a small hill, her board tilting left and then right as she swung back and forth to keep her speed down.

"I know about Evan!" I shouted after her, and she lost her balance, hit the curb on her right side, and went sprawling into the front lawn there. I winced and hurried to catch up to her.

"Ow. Jeez," she mumbled, sitting up and examining a

small scrape on her right forearm. "Warn me next time."

I went to retrieve her board from where it'd flipped over by the curb, then came back to her and offered her my hand. She took it, grimaced, and then let me pull her to her feet. I handed her the board. "Imagine *my* reaction," I told her.

"I should've texted you," she mumbled. "Just kind of panicked. I didn't want you to be mad." She nodded toward the street and started to walk, and I fell into step beside her.

"Why would I be mad?"

"Because we're all friends and now we've screwed things up."

"Do you like him?" I asked her abruptly. I wanted to get it out of the way early. Rip off the bandage, so to speak.

She was silent for a moment. Then she said, "I don't know."

I scoffed, unwilling to take that for an answer. "You don't know? How do you not know? Either you like him or you don't. I mean, you obviously liked him enough to kiss him."

"I don't know..." she repeated, and sounded like she wanted to say more.

"What?" I asked knowingly. "Was it bad?"

"I don't know."

"Riley. Seriously?"

"It's embarrassing!" she shot back. "I don't want to say it."

"How many embarrassing stories about boys have I

shared with you?" I reminded her. "Remember the time I was fourteen and Alan Hart sneezed in my face right before we were about to kiss?"

She hid a smile at that. "Yeah."

"Unless Evan sneezed in your face, I don't want to hear you complain about not wanting to tell me."

"It's not about the kissing. It's about why I let him kiss me." She hesitated, and then stopped in her tracks suddenly, offering me her board. Confused, I took it from her. "Just carry it for me. It takes away the temptation to use it to get away from you."

"Gotcha." I tucked the board under my arm awkwardly, unfamiliar with how to carry it. Riley watched the ground as we walked.

"It's embarrassing because... I kind of just wanted..." She bit her lip. "Just wanted to be wanted."

"Oh." I furrowed my eyebrows, looking away from her. I didn't know what to make of that. Riley'd never seemed bothered by not having a boyfriend before. What had changed?

"And he was there. I'm not, like, blind or anything. I knew he had a crush on me... or at least that he used to. I just thought maybe if I never said anything and *he* never said anything, it wouldn't be weird and we could all just pretend we all only liked each other as friends. And now I've screwed all of that up over... I don't know. A dumb feeling, I guess."

"You've never complained about not dating anyone," I pointed out. "I thought you liked being single."

"I don't hate it. It's just..." She reddened visibly now,

and finished, "you went off with Josh, and I knew you were going to have this perfect night, and I felt kind of lonely, I guess." She exhaled sharply. "Told you it was embarrassing."

"Well, no need to worry, because my night was worse than yours," I told her. "Josh and I didn't have sex. Actually, we kind of did the opposite of that." She shot me a confused look and I elaborated, "We broke up."

"What? Why? You were so into him."

"The short version is that he's leaving and we don't want to do long distance. The long version is... well, *that* but with slightly more detail. It was mutual but it doesn't feel mutual, you know? But I'll be okay. I came here to talk about you."

"You and Josh dated for over a year, Kayla. That's way more important than a kiss with Evan."

"I know it was more than just one kiss," I corrected her, and she avoided my eyes. "And it's just as big of a deal, because it's Evan. He really likes you, and..." I swallowed hard and pushed forward. This was going to be the hardest part. "And if you want to try dating him, maybe you should. If you really like him, I mean."

"But what about you?" she asked.

"What *about* me?"

"It wouldn't be fair to you to make you, like, the third wheel. Especially after what's happened with you and Josh." She frowned a little, but it faded, and then she smiled over at me, amused. "Remember when we were twelve and we'd just built our shelter with Evan earlier that week, and we went and hung out in it for the first time together, just the two of us? And we talked about how neither of us would *ever* date Evan because first of all, we thought the idea was gross – especially you, after what happened at Madison Reed's party."

"Don't remind me, ugh," I replied with a shudder.

"And secondly, we said we didn't want anyone to be left out. I don't want to be the one to break that promise."

"Well, if one of us has to, it looks like you're gonna have to step up," I joked, "because it won't be me, that's for sure." When she didn't laugh, I glanced to her anxiously, wondering if I'd said the wrong thing. I didn't want to imply that dating Evan was gross if she was actually into him now. "I mean, not that he isn't good-looking, and obviously he's the best guy we know. He's just not my type. But if he's yours, that's okay."

"I don't know," she said again. "Like I said: I just didn't want to feel alone."

"You're not alone. You have Evan and me. You always will. Or you'll always have me, at least. You know that, right?"

"Yeah, I know. But I wanted more than friendship, and it was easy to just go with it at the time. I thought maybe..." she trailed off, and then seemed to change her mind about continuing. "I don't know."

I let out a sigh. The more I talked to her, the more it sounded like she didn't feel the same way about Evan that he felt about her. I began to wonder if that was better or worse than her returning his feelings. Evan was going to be crushed if she rejected him. I had to think about his feelings, too. "You know he's liked you for a really long time."

"I know," she groaned. "What should I do?"

I bit my lip and resisted the urge to heave another sigh. I'd already promised Evan I'd give it my best shot, and so I did what he'd asked me to. "You should do what you want to, of course, but... maybe you should give it a chance."

She arched an eyebrow at me, clearly surprised. "Are you serious?"

"Yeah," I insisted, feigning confidence. "I mean, you already love him more than you love any other guy we know, and you've kind of already taken the next step, so maybe the best thing to do is to just go with it."

"What if it's not like you or Evan thinks it'll be?" she asked. "What if... something goes wrong, or I'm not the kind of girlfriend he thought I'd be..." She shook her head. "It feels weird to even say. Evan's... I mean, he seemed like a brother. How am I supposed to be his girlfriend?"

"I couldn't do it," I agreed, and then winced inwardly at the fact that I'd slipped up yet again. This really wasn't getting any easier. "But, um, that doesn't mean you couldn't."

"You *really* think it's a good idea?" she pressed, looking over at me.

I looked back at her, straight into her eyes, and tried my best to be convincing. "Yeah, I really do. *Any* girl would be lucky to have Evan. And any guy would be lucky to have you. You two deserve each other."

"What about you? You wouldn't feel weird around us?

Or get upset? You're totally fine with this?"

"Of course it's fine. You guys are my best friends. It's, like, my mission to make sure you're both happy."

"But you *just* broke up with your boyfriend."

"So what? I'll find another. I always do. You shouldn't not date someone just because I'm single. I will be *totally* fine."

She faced forward again, and I could sense she was turning my words over in her head. "You *really* think so?" she asked again, and I rolled my eyes and shoved her lightly.

"Yes! Now stop asking!"

"Okay, okay." We slowed down as her house came into view, and I grabbed her hand and linked two of my fingers with two of hers, like we'd used to as kids. She squeezed my fingers and I squeezed back.

"I guess he loves me more than anyone else ever will," she mused. "Romantically, anyway."

I furrowed my eyebrows, realizing I'd hadn't thought of it that way until now. Riley and Evan were lifelong friends. If they really did fall in love, there was no beating that kind of history. If they really *did* fall in love... they were kind of perfect for each other.

"Probably," I agreed, and wondered why I had to try so hard not to sound sad about it. Things were going to be *fine.*

***

"Update: Things are NOT fine."

I typed out the message on my laptop and sent it to Vanessa. I could practically hear her laughter on the other end of our chat window as she wrote her reply.

"They're getting it on in front of you right now, aren't they?" she sent back.

I reached out and lowered the screen partially so that I could see over it. Evan and Riley were sitting just a few feet away on the other couch in my living room. They'd come over to watch a movie. We were three weeks into them testing the waters, and I was losing patience faster than I'd thought possible.

"Cuddling," I typed back to Vanessa.

Which they were. Evan had his arm around Riley and she was huddled into his side. They had a blanket over them, and I was watching them like a hawk to ensure none of their hands disappeared under it. I didn't know most of the details of the inner-workings of their sort-of-a-relationship yet, and I certainly had no intention of finding out.

"That's not even that bad. Chill," Vanessa sent back, and I logged off with a dismissive scoff, shutting my laptop down completely. She couldn't understand.

Evan and Riley weren't meant to be EvanandRiley. That much was clear to me, now that I'd had more time to think about the idea. They just... didn't *fit right*. And besides, it was very possible that regardless of how Riley felt about him, if I'd have told her not to date Evan, she'd have turned him down immediately, out of respect for our three-way friendship. So they were only really together on account of my blessing. Kayla giveth, and

Kayla taketh away.

Evan caught my eye and smiled at me – or positively beamed, more like – and I forced a smile back, then slouched down slightly in my chair. I was reminded of why I couldn't retract my blessing: because Evan was in actual paradise. And as much as I hated to admit it, Riley didn't seem miserable.

And technically, they weren't all that bad about PDA, if I was perfectly honest. I knew I was being overly sensitive. Even their handholding made me shudder when it caught me off-guard. I'd never even seen them kiss, let alone anything worse than that. It was almost like most of the differences in how they'd been as friends and how they were as a couple were either subtle or totally in my head.

But knowing that didn't really help me feel any better.

When the movie was over, Evan yawned, stretched, and then got to his feet. "That was good." He turned to Riley. "Ready to go?"

"Actually, she was gonna stay the night," I cut in. We'd planned this sleepover two weeks in advance, actually, just to ensure that Riley still spent a comparable amount of time with me to what she spent with Evan. Riley looked to me, alarmed, and then back to Evan.

"Oh, man. I totally forgot. Kayla, Evan and I were gonna go bowling."

"You can come too!" Evan added eagerly, but the hand he raised to awkwardly rub at the back of his head made it even more obvious that they hadn't planned on me joining them.

"No," Riley corrected, "I should stay with Kayla. I promised her first."

"No, no, no," I insisted, waving them away. I could take the good friend bullet. I'd been doing it a lot lately, anyway. "You guys go without me. Have your date thing or whatever."

Evan looked to Riley like he expected her to accept my offer, but she shook her head emphatically. "You're not getting rid of me. Evan, we can do it another night."

"You sure?" he asked, and I could tell he was disappointed.

"Yeah. Next weekend, okay?" She stood on her tiptoes to kiss him on the cheek, and avoided my eyes afterward, still clearly uncomfortable with kissing him in front of me. Or maybe with kissing him at all. A part of me unabashedly hoped it was the latter. "See you tomorrow."

"See you. Both of you," he added and waved goodbye to me.

Riley look absolutely mortified by the time the front door had shut behind him. "Oh my god. I'm *that* friend. I'm so sorry."

"You're not that friend," I sighed out. "Don't be so hard on yourself. You've never dated before. You should've gone with him."

"No way. I promised you first, and you're my friend, too."

"Evan's not your friend, Riley," I reminded her. "He's officially been elevated."

"Is that really how it works?" she asked. "What if I don't want to choose him over you?"

I shrugged my shoulders. "I don't know. I guess you have to find a balance."

"Okay, and I did. You tonight and him some other time." She walked to me and tugged me to her, and then, to my surprise, wrapped me up in a tight hug. "Don't let me do that again, okay? You're going way too easy on me."

"I was way worse with Josh," I reminded her.

"Yeah, but you guys..." she began, and then shook her head and released me. "Evan and I are different."

"But good?" I asked her, curious.

"Different," she repeated, glancing over her shoulder like she was worried she'd be overheard.

"What does that mean? It's not good?" I felt bad for getting a little giddy at the idea, and then even worse when I remembered Evan beaming at me just half an hour ago.

"No, it's, I mean... he's nice," she told me eagerly, but then her smile faded and she let go of my hand. "Anyway, let's do something. We should find another movie to watch."

I followed her – somewhat grudgingly – up to my bedroom to watch our second movie in there on my laptop. I sensed there was something she wasn't telling me, but I didn't want to pressure her to say it, and I wasn't sure I even wanted to know what it was. Maybe there was a good reason for her to keep it from me.

We turned on the movie and sprawled out on my bed,

both of us wearing pajamas from my dresser drawers, and I settled in beside her to watch, our arms pressed together between us. My bedroom felt a little warmer than usual.

"Have you still been talking to Josh?" she asked me quietly after a few minutes. I was surprised by the question, but I didn't show it.

"Yeah, a little. We still eat lunch at the same table. But it's kind of weird now. At least we don't hate each other or anything, I guess."

There was a long silence as we watched Jennifer Gardner's character wander around her apartment on my laptop screen, and then Riley asked, "Do you think it'd be like that with me and Evan?"

I shrugged my shoulders, eager to talk about anything but Evan right now. Even silence was preferable. "No idea."

"Do you want us to break up?"

"Stop," I scoffed. "C'mon, this is just getting good. Mark Ruffalo's gonna show up soon."

"That wasn't an answer."

"Okay, here's one: no, now can we talk about anything *other* than Evan?"

"Sorry," she mumbled, and I sighed.

"No, I'm sorry. I'm just having a rough time dealing with the whole Josh thing. I shouldn't take it out on you." It wasn't *entirely* untrue.

She reached out for my hand and cuddled up to me. "Well, we're doing this special event thing at the skate park later this week after school. It's just a bunch of us showing off, basically. It's super casual. You should come watch."

I knew without asking that Evan was coming too and considered turning her down. Then I wondered how I'd so quickly let myself start to actively avoid Riley and Evan when they were together. Before, I'd been well aware that they spent more time with each other than they did with me, but that'd been okay. We'd all still been best friends, and I'd also had an entirely different set of friends to keep me busy.

Now I was out a boyfriend – something my mom was *still* pressing me for details about, nearly a month later – and the idea of hanging out with Riley and Evan simultaneously was anything but pleasant. And now it bothered me that they saw each other more than they saw me.

"What day is your thing?" I asked her.

"Wednesday."

"Okay," I decided. I could suck it up for an afternoon. "I'll come."

She grinned and squeezed me tight. "Thank you." Then she leaned in and pressed a quick kiss to my cheek. That was new.

I glanced to her to see that she'd already turned to face the movie on my laptop again, and so I mimicked the action, watching Jennifer Gardner and Mark Ruffalo reconnect for the first time since childhood. I wondered if that'd be me and Riley one day: steadily growing apart until one day we'd just be old friends bumping into each other for a few seconds before we went back to our daily lives. Maybe *I'd* be an old friend but *Evan* would be her husband. The thought made my heart ache.

I couldn't lose Riley. I loved Evan dearly, but if I had to, I knew I'd choose her over him, and I knew he'd do the same. But what scared me was that I didn't know who she'd choose.

I wondered why I was so sure it was a choice she'd eventually have to make.

***

Wednesday, Evan drove Riley and me to the skate park, and we sat with a group a few feet away from The Pit, a large hole in the ground filled with ramps and rails to skate on and over. Riley joined us to watch the first few skaters who were brave enough to show off in front of the crowd that'd gathered, and I told her, "That looks cute on you. You should wear them more often."

"What, this?" she asked, pointing to the gray beanie on her head. I nodded, and she grinned. "Thanks. I've had it since Christmas but I haven't worn it. I'm trying to get some use out of it before it gets too hot."

"Well, it's cute," I repeated, not sure what else to say. She looked good. I hadn't come here with her more than a few times, and each time she looked more and more at home. I liked seeing her in her element.

"Glad you think so."

"I like your hair, though," Evan commented from my other side. "That thing covers up like half your head."

"Well, good thing I don't care what boys think," Riley

shot back, and I relaxed between them, grinning. Moments like these, where they bantered back and forth like they always had, gave me hope that maybe things could still be normal even if they were dating.

"You don't care what I think? But I'm your boyfriend."

My smile dropped. Evan was not in the mood for friendly banter, it seemed.

"And Kayla has better fashion sense. She overrules you."

"Yes, I do." I nudged her and gestured to The Pit while Evan sighed, and we actively made an effort to ignore him. "You should take a shot at it. Or is it too crowded?"

"I don't like skating in front of a lot of people," Riley admitted. "Dylan and Brett kind of talked me into coming today. They're right there." She pointed to two boys I recognized, who were perched at the lip of The Pit, one foot on their boards. Even as I watched, one of them tipped his board forward and then went rolling down the ramp, where he pushed forward until he reached a rail. He jumped, taking the board with him, and slid along the rail for several feet before jumping down and sticking the landing.

"Whoa," I said, taken aback. "He's really good."

"I can do that," Riley told me. "When I'm by myself, at least."

"Why haven't you ever shown me?" I asked. "Or *anyone*? It's a total turn-on. Dylan and Brett should be all over you if they see you do this all the time." Evan tensed up beside me and I didn't acknowledge it.

Neither did Riley, who laughed at what I'd said. "Yeah,

right. A turn-on. Just like purple hair?"

"I like your hair," I said, and then pushed lightly at her leg. "Go! I wanna see."

"Me too," added Evan, half-heartedly.

"Alright. I'll go. But when I embarrass myself you guys are taking me out to lunch or paying my medical bills... whichever is more of a necessity when I'm done here."

"Deal," I agreed, and Evan raised his hand to his mouth to chew nervously at a fingernail. I grabbed at his wrist. "Stop that."

"I can't. Nervous habit."

"I know, dummy, I've known you for ten years. Chill out; Riley's been doing this for almost as long as you've known your multiplication tables."

"Remember that time I broke an arm on the school playground and he started hyperventilating?" Riley asked, and we shared a laugh at Evan's expense while he reddened beside me.

"Okay, I get it. I'll calm down," he muttered.

"Good luck. But I'm sure you won't need it," I told Riley. She took off her beanie and tossed it to me, replacing it with a helmet. Then she laid her board down onto the ground, skated to the edge of The Pit, and without further ado, let herself drop down the side ramp. I noticed as she joined the other skaters that she was the only girl.

But that wasn't the only thing that made her stand out. She soared across to the ramp on the other side, gaining speed, then sped up the side of it at nearly a ninety-degree angle, got at least half a foot of air, and then twisted around, gripping her board with one hand, to drop back down the ramp and swing back around to the other side.

One of the boys she'd pointed to earlier – Brett or Dylan, I wasn't sure – stuck two fingers into his mouth and whistled at her. Evan and I exchanged impressed looks, his moodiness momentarily forgotten. She was *awesome*.

"Did you know she could do that?" I asked him, and he shook his head.

"No. I'm guessing you didn't either?"

"No clue."

"Jeez, what else isn't she telling us?" Evan asked. We watched Riley skate over to the boy who'd whistled so she could high-five him. Then he wrapped an arm around her to pull her to him in a casual hug, and Evan added, "Do you think she dated him and just never told us?"

"I've asked. Unless she lied to me, they're just friends. And I don't think she'd lie."

"I guess not." He fell silent, but I could sense he was still a little uneasy. He was getting fidgety again.

"A word of advice, Evan," I told him. "Don't get possessive. I'd dump you in an instant if you got possessive."

"Good thing Riley's not you," he mumbled, and I resisted the urge to respond. I managed to hold off for about two seconds.

"Don't be such a jerk. I helped you out with getting together with her, remember?"

"That doesn't mean you know everything. And you know, I don't even get why you came. You aren't into this."

"Oh, and you *are?*"

"I'm into *her.* It's basically the same thing. This was supposed to be something the two of us did together. She only invited you because you made her feel bad the other night."

"Are you kidding me right now?" I asked him, appalled. He stared straight ahead, refusing to look at me. "I told her to go bowling with you! She chose to stay and sleep over."

"I'm just saying, you don't have to crash just for the sake of crashing. We aren't gonna stop being friends with you just because we're together. Loosen up."

"Oh, *I'm* the one who needs to loosen up. Okay." I stood and threw Riley's beanie at him. "Enjoy your *date.* God knows you two need more time alone without me; it's not like you don't get it *every other day.*"

I stormed away and made it about one hundred feet before I realized I didn't have a ride home. So instead, I paused, gritted my teeth, and fumed in place, angry with Evan and also with myself. The right thing to do had been to tell Riley how I really felt from the beginning. Now I felt like it was too late.

"Kayla, wait."

I recognized Evan's voice and tensed. "I don't want to talk to you."

"I'm sorry. I'm just super paranoid, okay?"

I rounded on him to see him running a frustrated

66

hand through his hair. "That's no reason to take it out on me."

"I know. It's just... I look at me, and I see this awkward, lanky guy whose best quality is that he's good at math. And then I look at Riley. And I know that I'm the luckiest guy on earth to be her friend, let alone her boyfriend. It's like it's too good to be true. I'm looking over my shoulder wondering what's gonna make it all come crashing down, and I need to remember that you're not the enemy."

"No, you need to remember that there *is* no enemy. You keep acting like this and you'll deserve to be dumped," I spat at him.

"I know. Don't go. Riley wouldn't want us to fight, and neither do I."

"You started it," I reminded him.

"I know," he repeated. "Please stay. You're right. This is a fun thing for all of us, and I'm being an ass. It's not my place to hog our friend. Even if I am dating her." He watched me, silently pleading, as I stared back with my arms folded across my chest.

At last, I told him, "You're paying for *my* lunch, too."

"Done."

Grudgingly, I rejoined him, and he wrapped an arm around my shoulders, letting out a heavy breath. "I just feel like I'm on some prank show and any second now someone's gonna jump out and reveal this was all a joke, you know?" he said. "This is just taking some getting used to."

"Yes, it certainly is," I agreed stiffly, and shrugged his

arm off my shoulder.

Chapter Four

I spent Josh's graduation day at home alone, flicking through old pictures of the two of us on my phone. It'd been two months since our break-up, and the whole thing still felt like one big open wound in my chest.

And it seemed likely that it was going to stay open for a while. Given that Riley and Evan weren't exactly the best people to be around when I was feeling miserable about my old relationship, Vanessa was the obvious choice to help cheer me up. And she was going to be visiting family in France for the entirety of the summer, without even a cell phone to use to talk to me. Her parents didn't want her racking up charges for international calls.

That meant that I had no one but Riley and Evan to look forward to until my sister came home. And while they weren't absolutely horrific to be around, they weren't as fun as they'd used to be.

For one: the past couple of weekends, we'd taken our movie-watching habit out of my house and to the movie theater. We saw two movies on two different weekends. During the first, I sat alone with my solo bucket of popcorn while my two best friends sat close together, shared their own bucket, and mostly ignored me, though that last past was kind of Evan's fault. Riley always tried her best to spread the love when the three of us were together, but Evan wasn't a great sharer.

When I dropped the hint to Riley afterward that I wasn't really feeling the whole movie thing given that they were a couple and I didn't have a boyfriend to bring along, she asked for one more shot. So we'd gone to the second movie a week later, where we'd all shared one bucket of popcorn and Riley'd spent most of it whispering to me rather than to Evan, much to his displeasure. Everything was all squared away.

That would've satisfied any normal friend, but given that I'd developed a case of raging jealousy over their couple status and my own solid status as a third wheel, I was no normal friend. And I'd noticed the way Evan had insisted upon holding Riley's hand throughout the entire duration of the second movie. I vowed to turn down any future movie offers.

I couldn't even be sure if I was actually overreacting anymore, because Evan had turned into such a stage ten clinger that I felt my only option was to be just as stubborn. I'd settle for nothing less than things being just like they'd been for the past ten years. I wanted the Riley back that linked half of her fingers with mine and smiled at me like I'd made her whole day with one lame joke.

And make no mistake, this *was* about Riley. Evan and I were best friends, but she was my *best* friend and she was also his. I was jealous that they both had someone to date, sure, but I was also jealous that Evan was getting more attention from her than I was.

This current arrangement wasn't how our triangle was supposed to work. He always gotten more time with her, sure, but the time she and I got was more personal. He got a few hours at the creek every other day and I got a shared bed and the chance to spend all night talking about anything and everything with her.

Those nights were rare now. Everything with Riley was rare now. I was practically invested in making it so, because where Riley went, Evan went, and the two of them weren't fun to be around. Mostly because Evan wasn't fun to be around. Their whole fling had done awful things to his personality.

Not long after summer began, Nicole finally came home from college, which was pretty much my saving grace. She'd just finished up her freshman year and had all kinds of hilarious and interesting stories, and I very quickly latched onto her, both because I loved hanging out with her and because it provided me with an easy, believable excuse to get some much-needed time away from the unit that was EvanandRiley.

Nicole took me to the mall her first week back, and

when we stopped at the food court for lunch, she told me, "Oh, so I have a story I think you'll like. Remember my roommate I told you about? Not the two I don't really hang out with but the one I told you I really liked?"

"Yeah, what was her name? Gretchen, or something?" I guessed.

"Grace," Nicole corrected. "Anyway, she's like the best friend I made this year and part of what I liked about her was that she was the only roommate who wasn't *constantly* bringing guys home. I mean, I made guy friends that I brought over sometimes but our other two roommates were in sororities and it got pretty ridiculous."

"*You're* in a sorority," I reminded her, grinning.

"Yes, but I don't sleep around like they did. That's not the point, anyway. So Grace goes nearly the whole year and I never see her with any guys romantically, and she doesn't bring any around other than a couple who were obviously just friends of hers. And she and I are like really close at this point. Then, two weeks before finals, I come home earlier than she expected me to while she had the apartment to herself, and she's making out with a *girl* on our couch. Evidently, I have really bad gaydar! And that's the story of how I didn't know my new best friend was a lesbian. For an entire year."

I laughed at her and then asked, "She didn't say anything all year?"

"Well, from what she told me, she came from a really rural area where she never told anyone, and I think it made her too freaked to say anything, even in college.

Obviously we were all nice about it, though. I've discovered since then that she actually might be the most promiscuous of us all; she was just better at hiding it. Which is hilarious and amazing. You'll meet her in a couple of weeks when she comes up with a few other people for my birthday."

"Cool. Oh, what do you want?" I asked her, glad she'd brought it up while we were in the mall. "I want to get you something you'll actually like."

"Don't worry about it. You should just surprise me. Anyway, how's your year been? Other than Josh, of course." She paused, and then pointed out, "I heard from *you* about your breakup, but I had to hear about Riley and Evan from Mom. Why didn't you tell me?"

"Ugh, because the less I have to talk about that, the better." I shook my head at her with a roll of my eyes.

"They're that bad?"

"Not Riley. I mean, you know how she is. She'd never purposely want me to feel left out. But I think Evan's so in love he wants to spend every waking moment with her."

"Well, he'll suffocate her and then they'll break up," Nicole said, shrugging her shoulders. "Problem solved."

"No, because then things will be awkward and instead of fighting to get time alone with either of them, I'll be fighting to get them to be in each other's presence for more than two minutes." I sighed. "Whatever; I deserve it. It's my fault this started."

"You did the whole 'whatever makes you happy' thing, didn't you?" asked Nicole, a knowing look on her face. I

73

nodded pitifully. "No, never *ever* do that. Story time—"

"Again?" I asked with a laugh.

"Listen. In high school, my friend Terri asked me if she should date this guy named Derek. Now, I get the whole pot thing on a casual level, but he was a massive stoner – we're talking daily, here – and was flunking half of his classes. I bent over backwards making sure *that* couple never happened. And now Derek busses tables at this very mall and probably spends half his paycheck on weed, and Terri's dating a Computer Science major over at CWU."

"Well, Evan doesn't do drugs, unfortunately, so I'm just gonna have to wait for Riley to get sick of him and then try to mend it afterwards. What else can I do?"

"Sabotage it," Nicole answered far too casually.

I laughed. "No way. Not an option."

"Well, then, you would be correct: your job is to put up with them until it's time to pick up the pieces."

"And this would be why I'm avoiding them and going to the mall with you."

She grinned at me. "Nice. Way to make me feel appreciated. But in all seriousness, you can't avoid them until they break up. They could date for years."

The thought sent a shudder down my spine. "Well, I can try."

***

My mom and Nicole went out to get manicures and pedicures around noon a few days later, and I turned down the offer to join them, feeling a little off. I knew through social media that Riley and Evan had gone to the movies the night before without me, and I'd surprised myself by getting a little teary when I'd found out. I couldn't pinpoint why I was *that* upset, given that if they'd invited me I'd have turned them down anyway, but I was.

I laid sprawled out on my bed with headphones in and my phone in my hand, watching my ceiling as the music blasted in my ears just loudly enough to block out all other noise. I closed my eyes and just enjoyed not thinking for a few minutes. Because Vanessa wasn't around, whenever Nicole couldn't find the time to keep me company I found myself alone, stuck in my own head. I was the one avoiding my best friends, but that didn't stop my brain from telling me things like *"They don't miss you"* and *"They never liked you that much anyway"* and *"They only need each other now"* and *"They don't mind that you're avoiding them"*.

I was jolted back to reality by the feeling of movement on my bed. Two hands grabbed my wrists and pinned them, and I opened my eyes, my heart shooting up into my throat, only to see a grinning Riley hovering over me.

"Oh my god," I squeaked out, and then paused my music when I couldn't even hear my own voice. She was giggling by the time I could hear again. "You scared the crap out of me."

"I couldn't resist," she admitted. "I'm guessing your mom and sister aren't home? Thanks for telling me Nicole's back, by the way. I just saw her car in the driveway."

"You were busy," I said, not looking her in the eyes.

"You're avoiding me," she replied, hands still on my wrists. I realized how close we were and squirmed uncomfortably, and she let me go with a sigh, sitting back on my bed. I sat up as she added, "Don't deny it."

"I'm not avoiding you," I said, and she groaned at me.

"Okay, cut it out. I talked to Evan, alright? I got the message, and so did he, even if he wanted to pretend not to. We are going to act *exactly* the same as we did before we started dating. You're gonna forget we're a couple. If we remind you at all that we are, you reserve the right to terminate our hangout and start avoiding us again. We miss you." She paused, and then asked, somewhat shyly, "I mean, that *was* all that was bothering you, right? The third-wheel thing?"

"Yeah," I replied, confused. "What else would be bothering me?"

"Nothing," she said hastily. "I just wanted to be sure I covered all the bases."

"Well, I have a hard time believing Evan's as committed to making me feel better as you are."

"I know. So I told him I'd dump him if he didn't do this with me."

"Harsh," I declared, surprised. "You did that for me?"

"Of course. Believe it or not, being alone with Boyfriend Evan isn't as fun as hanging out with Friend Evan and you. Especially when I know you're off somewhere alone and purposely not coming with us the times we invite you."

"Can I ask you something?" I replied, eyebrows furrowed.

She collapsed beside me on the bed, arms crossed behind her head. "Shoot."

"You aren't as into him as he's into you."

There was a pause. "...That wasn't a question."

"So you're not even gonna deny it?"

She shrugged her shoulders, though she looked a little uncomfortable. "I guess not. I mean, he liked me first."

"But you *did* like him back," I confirmed. "When you asked me if you should date him, you wanted to."

"I don't know. I was thinking about it." She sighed. "I'm having trouble being able to tell the difference between having a crush on someone and just wanting attention. Because I'm an awful person."

"You're not," I told her. "Everyone wants to feel wanted. The goal is kind of to feel wanted by someone who feels wanted by you back, though. Maybe..." I hesitated. It hadn't occurred to me that this was the case before I'd been about to say it, but now that it was in my head, I felt surprisingly confident that I was onto something. "Maybe that's why Evan's going crazy. He doesn't feel as wanted back as he'd like to."

"I spend a ton of time with him," Riley laughed. "Sometimes more than I can take."

"Maybe he can tell it's more than you can take. People pick up on that kind of stuff, you know?"

"You know, before I started dating one, boys always seemed so simple," said Riley. "They were even easier to make friends with than girls were. Just talk about video games and tell them I skate, and boom, done."

"I never realized I'm your only female friend," I told her, taken aback by the revelation.

"You are," she confirmed. "But maybe I only need one." She rolled toward me and wrapped an arm over my stomach, pulling me down onto the bed and cuddling into my side. "Don't let this whole thing with Evan get to you, okay? I'd die if I lost you."

"Morbid," I mumbled as she kissed me on the cheek again. She'd never really done that growing up, and I wondered if being affectionate with Evan had just brought that side out of her. I wasn't sure how to feel about it. The feeling I got when she did it wasn't unpleasant, but it wasn't comfortable, either.

Later, I'd refer to this day – the day I spent several hours just lying on my bed, napping with Riley at my side – as Epiphany Day. As I lay there in silence with Riley pressed into me, her eyes closed and her breathing tickling my neck and her arm around me and her fingers tangled gently with mine, my heart squeezed itself tighter in my chest. I glanced down to where Riley's head rested, and she tilted her face downward slightly, which made her lips brush against my collarbone. I noticed her eyes had closed.

When I was eight, I'd bent over and ripped my tights in front of an entire crowd of family and friends who'd come to see a few of us in my gymnastics class perform. When I was eleven, I'd taken a small tumble off of a water ride, and they'd had to shut it down while they carried me out on a stretcher in front of nearly a hundred disappointed people who'd been waiting to go on the ride.

Both of those moments were less uncomfortable than this one.

I cursed Nicole for putting the idea of lesbianism into my head such a short time ago in the first place, because now it was fresh and, for some bizarre reason, my mind had gone there, and I was thinking about my best childhood friend and me while she was pressed up against me, which was pretty much the last thing I'd ever thought I'd be thinking about. Up until about thirty seconds ago, I'd have believed I'd willingly imagine, in detail, the entirety of a threesome with Evan and Josh before I'd ever let the idea of Riley and me even cross my mind.

And my mind didn't stop there. The stupid little voice I knew to be my conscience suggested that maybe I was being so over the top about Riley and Evan because it wasn't just about the change to the dynamics of our joint friendship. Maybe I had feelings for one of them. And, even worse, maybe I had feelings for the one that wasn't a boy.

I scoffed aloud and Riley didn't react, so I assumed she was no longer fully conscious. I wasn't *gay*. There was no way. Like, there was the "no way am I gay" in the closet-case sort of way, where full-on denial was very clearly happening, and then there was *my* "no way am I gay," which was entirely and whole-heartedly legitimate. I liked boys, and I'd liked them for as long as I could remember. There was zero doubt in my mind that my feelings for Josh and each and every one of the boys before him had been real.

So I couldn't be gay. It was natural to want to experiment in college, so maybe I was just ahead of the curve. Riley would've certainly been the ideal candidate, if I *had* to kiss a girl. She was hot. I was allowed to acknowledge that my best female friend was hot, and it was probably normal for my brain to float the idea of hooking up with her at *some* point, given that aforementioned hotness.

Just because it wasn't talked about often didn't mean that *occasionally* thinking about other girls wasn't a thing. Nicole'd probably thought about it with her gay roommate. It didn't mean that I liked girls.

This was nothing a quick Google search couldn't cure, so later that night, after Riley left, I got onto my laptop and searched "jealous of my best friends dating". Then I praised myself for getting the idea in the first place. Not only would this prove that what I felt was totally normal (and didn't mean I necessarily had romantic feelings for Riley *or* for Evan), but there was a chance it'd also help me find a way to get over it.

I frowned as I scrolled through the results. "I'm jealous of my boyfriend's best friend," was one. That wasn't what I was looking for. There were a lot more that were similar to that one. Another was titled "20 Signs You're Actually Dating Your BFF". I was very careful to avoid clicking that one.

After being put off by how rare my situation seemed to be according to the internet, at last, I found one that seemed relevant. Someone with the initials "LH" asked: "I'm 18 and male and my best friend has started dating a girl we've both been friends with for a while. I can't help but feel jealous of their relationship and like he won't have time for me anymore because he's just focusing on her. I'm very attached to him, and I don't know why this pisses me off so much, but is this normal? Anyone else ever dealt with this?"

I scrolled down to the first response. "Had this scenario once before but I was the one who started dating my friend and my other friend got jealous. So this is definitely a thing that happens." I paused there, relieved. I was normal. It was nice to have it finally confirmed.

I read on. "But when it happened to me, it turned out my friend had a crush on me. Is it possible you could be gay and attracted to your best friend?"

I scoffed loudly, feeling my face heat up. "*Seriously*? C'mon!"

I skimmed through the rest of the responses. "There is nothing wrong with being gay. Just admit it." "Dude, you're gay." "Hella gay." "Does LH stand for 'latent homosexual'?" "Move to San Francisco and make new 'friends'." The only one that wasn't some variation of a gay joke was: "You're being irrational. Stop being a bad friend and feel happy for your best friend because he is obviously with someone who makes him happy."

"Thanks, internet," I snapped. "I'm either an awful friend, gay, or both. Real helpful." I closed my laptop, fuming, and let out a heavy sigh, wishing I'd never gotten the idea to look in the first place.

I hadn't talked to Josh much since we'd stopped seeing each other, but now I wondered if I'd done the right thing by turning him down that night in the hotel room. If Riley and Evan were going to spend the summer making out and maybe even hooking up, why was I stopping myself from doing the same? And why not take it a step further? Nicole's roommates had spent the year having casual sex, according to her, so why couldn't I? I'd probably be doing it anyway in just a couple of years.

Josh, of course, wasn't the ideal guy to hook up with. There were too many feelings there for it to truly be casual, and my aim wasn't to get myself hurt. But Nicole's birthday was in ten days, and she had college boys coming up for the night.

"Gay, my ass," I mumbled, and tossed my laptop to the other side of my bed, far too excited about my new plan to go to sleep. Instead, I stayed up for another hour thinking about what I wanted to wear if I was going to look my best.

For the boys, of course. Always the boys.

Chapter Five

Riley and Evan talked me into coming over to Evan's the following Saturday, and I agreed to give them a chance to make good on Riley's promise. This was their first opportunity to try out acting like normal friends around me.

I liked the idea in theory, but in practice, I was second-guessing it. I knew they'd just be pretending. It bothered me to see them act like a couple because it bothered me that they *were* a couple. But I couldn't tell Riley that. Not after the other day. Not when I was determined to convince myself that if I just stopped being treated like a third wheel I'd stop caring that I was one.

I took longer than usual to get ready. I was a face-full-of-makeup kind of girl even when I was just hanging out with Riley and Evan. At the least, I usually needed some light foundation. So I was always the last one ready when it came to Riley, Evan, and me going out or doing anything together – which tended to annoy both of them to no end.

But today was different. I didn't want to put make-up on just because it made me feel presentable. I wanted to impress. *Who* I wanted to impress, I wasn't sure. It was just Evan and Riley. Neither of them would look at me twice. But I still didn't want to show up looking... typical.

On the other hand, I'd also been told to bring a bikini, so I knew that they probably wanted to take a trip to our neighborhood pool at some point today. It had just opened for the summer, so that wasn't surprising. But it also meant swimming, and swimming meant getting wet. Which meant getting dolled up was pointless. I'd have to settle for mediocre.

I pulled my hair up into a ponytail and examined it from several different angles to make sure it looked okay, and then I grabbed a bikini, slipped on a pair of flip-flops, and began the walk to Evan's house. Riley'd already texted me that she was there, so when I arrived, I made sure to ring the doorbell rather than just barging in like I normally would've. I didn't want to interrupt anything.

There wasn't an answer at first. I stood on the front porch awkwardly, waiting, and then, when there was still no response, I rang the doorbell again.

No sooner had I finished pressing the button than the front door suddenly swung open with more force than I'd expected. Evan was on the other side, and he was focused on the barely-visible television in the other room rather than on me. The second he'd gotten the door open, his hand left the doorknob and shot back to the gaming controller in his hand. "I said to pause it! Only the first player can!" he shouted.

Riley's laughter carried from the living room. "No way! I'm two zombies away from passing your body count!"

"Sorry Kayla," Evan said to me hastily, still not looking at me. "*Zombie Guts 3*'s versus mode gets kind of intense."

"I can see that," I replied, both amused and relieved. Of *course* they'd failed to come to the door because they'd both been absorbed in their video game. They were notorious for it. I'd never really gotten into video games like they were, but I liked watching them play together. Or at least I'd used to, because it'd been fun to fuel their rivalry from the sidelines. I wasn't sure it'd be the same now.

I stepped inside and closed the door behind myself; Evan was already rushing back into the living room and retaking his spot on the gaming chair directly in front of the television. I joined Riley on the couch and set my bikini down on the armrest. She shot me a quick grin and then went back to mashing buttons. Onscreen, the female character on the top half of the split screen hacked at a mob of zombies with a samurai sword.

"No fair; you got the sword!" Evan complained. "I was going for that! You only know where to find it because I told you!"

"Everyone knows the *Zombie Guts* creators always hide swords in the kitchen ovens. I would've found it anyway; there's only one house on this whole map. One house, one oven, one sword!" A serious of sound effects blared from the television suddenly, and the top half of the screen faded to green as the bottom slowly turned red. The green half bore the word "VICTORY", the red half, "DEFEAT". "Ha!" Riley teased, pumping a fist victoriously while Evan scoffed in front of us.

"That round doesn't count. There was interference."

"More like I won a battle of wills. You gave in and answered the door first."

"Because it's *my* house!"

"Whatever. I still won. But you can play again." She offered her controller to me. "Kayla, you should try. We can walk you through it."

"I can watch," I insisted. "You guys play again."

"No way." Riley forced the controller into my hands, and then said to Evan, "Put it on campaign mode." She turned back to me. "The game has a multiplayer campaign, but it's only for two players. You can either play as Gregor, this boring muscly dude with a Russian accent, or-"

"Hey! Gregor's amazing. You just don't like him because he's a guy," Evan interrupted.

"Well, the other option is Lila, and she runs around in combat boots and dual-wields pistols when you start out."

"Gregor starts off with a machine gun," Evan added helpfully. "But you can have Lila. We haven't finished the whole campaign yet, but I'm pretty sure they're supposed to be dating. We'll probably find out more as the story goes on."

"Ew! They're not dating! Lila would never! I think we're gonna find out they're related."

"No way! Lila isn't even Russian."

I looked back and forth between them, growing only more confused as Riley began to gesture to the buttons on the controller and explain what each button did. "Maybe we should play a board game," I said at last, and they both laughed like I was kidding.

Evan started the first level and we found ourselves in the center of a foggy wooded area. I heard groaning and then the sound of hurried footsteps, and then the word "RUN" blinked on and off on my screen. I saw Evan's character rush past mine. "Wait, which thumbstick do I use to go?" I asked, and then watched my character look up to the sky when I pressed a thumbstick forward. The zombie sound effects grew louder, and then the screen began to blink red as my controller vibrated. "GUTTED," the game told me a moment later, and Evan and Riley dissolved into giggles.

"Okay, board game it is," Riley agreed, and as Evan got up to go sift through the closet in which his family kept their extensive game collection, it certainly *felt* like we were all just friends again on the outside.

Now if only my insides could catch up.

***

The pool was less crowded than I thought it'd be for a hot Saturday in the summer. There were a few families around, which meant that the shallow end of the pool was filled with parents and their toddlers, but the deep end was entirely deserted. It took Evan less than a minute after we'd arrived to cannonball into the water.

"You forgot sunscreen!" Riley called to him once he resurfaced. She finished rubbing some into her arms, shoulders, and stomach, and then offered the bottle to me so I could do the same to myself.

"Dammit," I heard Evan say from within the pool. "Well, tell me when you guys are done with it and I'll get out."

"I'm done except for my back," I said.

"Me too. Do mine?" Riley asked me, already moving her hair out of the way and twisting away from me on the poolside recliner we shared.

"Oh. Yeah, sure." Uncomfortable, I squirted out a glob of sunscreen onto my hands, hesitated for a moment, and then began to rub it into her back. I'd done it at least a dozen times before, but suddenly it felt like a *thing*. I hoped it was just me and that it didn't feel weird to her. Or at least that she couldn't *tell* that I was feeling weird.

Evan wolf-whistled at us, grinning, and Riley told him, "Don't be an ass." I stopped abruptly even though I wasn't quite finished, unable to keep going after Evan's teasing. I was sure my face was turning red.

"It should be good enough."

"Thanks." Riley turned back to me and then motioned for me to turn away from her, which I gladly did, if only to avoid having to look her in the eyes. I heard Evan getting out of the water a moment later as she rubbed the sunscreen into my back. Her hands were softer than I remembered, and I knew I was overanalyzing way too much right around the time I wondered if they'd lingered on me for a few seconds after she'd finished or if I'd just imagined they had.

"Who's getting my back?" Evan asked us, and Riley tossed him the bottle dismissively.

"Get your own back."

"But you guys did each other," he argued as he moved to dry his torso off with a towel. Riley stood, ignoring him, and then took a running leap into the water. I took pity on him and hastily slathered a layer of sunscreen onto his back once he was dry. "Thanks."

"No problem," I told him, and then glanced past him to make sure Riley wasn't listening before I added, "Thanks for trying today."

"It's actually surprisingly effortless," he told me. "I like dating Riley, but I kinda forgot how much I liked all of us being friends. I think it's better this way."

I smiled at him, relieved to hear it. "Me too. Obviously."

He grinned back, then set the sunscreen aside and offered me his hand. "Let's get Riley."

I grabbed his hand in silent agreement, and together, we rushed to the pool and leapt in, aiming right for a foot in front of Riley, who saw us coming too late and hastily shielded her face with her hands before the splash we made swallowed her whole.

"You guys are evil! I hate you!" she spluttered out when she came up to the surface again, and Evan and I exchanged another look of understanding before we both sent a wave of water crashing toward her. She splashed us back a few times, trying valiantly to fight us off, and then I felt sorry for her and turned on Evan, leaping onto him to send him underwater while Riley laughed at us.

We fooled around like that for a while, and for the next few hours, though I remained aware that they were together and that I was single, I felt a little less lonely.

But come the next day, when they were *still* together and I was *still* single, the searing ache in my chest I'd been feeling for so long had returned, and I knew that it wasn't going to go away until I did something about it.

The problem was that I didn't know what that something was supposed to be.

***

I'd never met any of the friends Nicole had over for her birthday party, but I'd heard about most of them from her at some point, and when she introduced the seven of them, I retained about half of their names. There were four girls and three boys, and I only thought one of the boys was cute: a guy named Michael who'd just finished out his freshman year as well. As far as I knew, they were all upcoming sophomores, with the exception of one of the guys, who looked a little bit too old to be under 21.

The girl Nicole had told me about at the mall, Grace, seemed nice, but she and I didn't exchange more than a quick greeting before she'd gone back to talking to one of the other girls.

"They hooked up once," Nicole would tell me about the two girls later. "They're kind of off and on again, but never official. It's kind of complicated."

Despite my own hot and cold relationship with "EvanandRiley", I invited them to come to the party, figuring I'd be glad I had some company of my own once my mom went to bed and the alcohol inevitably came out.

And come out, it did.

Nicole and her friends took the party outside so that Mom wouldn't overhear, and once a few drinks had been poured, Evan headed into the fray to grab a couple for Riley and me, and then another for himself. We retreated to the edge of the action afterward, watching Nicole and her friends dance around to music from a portable stereo one of the boys brought.

"Which one was the one you thought was cute?" Riley asked me, and I pointed Michael out. He was dancing with Grace in this intentionally awkward way while she tossed her head back and laughed. I noticed then that she was kind of pretty, and forced my gaze back to Michael.

"You should go talk to him," Evan suggested, and when Riley gave him a warning look, he insisted, "I mean it! Not so we can be alone, but because you deserve to have a little fun."

"My thoughts exactly," I agreed and proceeded to down half of my drink. Riley looked nervous when I finished.

"You don't know him," she reminded me.

"Yeah, but they're Nicole's friends," I pointed out. "I trust her judgment. You don't think he's cute?"

"No," she said, and I rolled my eyes at her.

"Whatever. You're just trying to take the wind out of my sails. Why should I have to sit around all summer alone and miserable while you two enjoy having someone to date? I should be allowed to hook up."

"Nobody said you couldn't. But what happened to caring about what you do with your body?" Riley asked. "You ended your longest relationship rather than have sex with someone you knew it wouldn't work out with. Now you're all 'YOLO' because Evan and I are dating?"

"Yes." I nodded, then quickly finished the rest of my drink. "Seeing you two together made me realize that life is short. I'm not going to be the girl who stood back and watched everyone else enjoy themselves without participating herself."

"And she's not even drunk yet," Evan marveled, glancing to Riley with amusement.

Riley, however, looked like laughing was the last thing on her mind. "You're being ridiculous."

"Whatever." I rolled my eyes at her. "I'm getting a drink."

I went back to pour myself another, and felt Nicole's hand on my back as I turned around with a full cup in my hand. "Hey, be careful," she told me. "You're definitely a lightweight. Dwayne and I are taking a trip to get more alcohol – he's the only one here over 21 – but if you need help while I'm gone, ask Grace, okay?"

I nodded at her and she pointed to Grace, who was no longer dancing with Michael, to make sure I knew who she was. Grace was ready and offered me a quick smile and a wave before she turned back to resume talking to the other girl Nicole said she'd had a thing with. I watched them for a moment, curious. It didn't seem obvious that they were together, or had been together, or wanted to be together, or *whatever* it was they were. In fact, they looked a little tense.

I accidentally bumped into Michael on my way back to Evan and Riley, and grabbed at his arm to keep myself from falling. "Oh, man, I'm sorry. You're okay, right?" he asked me, placing a hand on my shoulder. I nodded at him, suddenly lacking the words to respond properly. He grinned down at me and asked, "You're Nicole's sister, right?"

"Yeah," I said, nodding again, and then added a hasty, "Nice to meet you," before I hurried away to rejoin my friends. It had taken me about five seconds to realize I was way too chicken to hold a conversation with a guy like Michael, let alone somehow convince him to hook up with me.

"Smooth," Evan told me when I reached him, smirking. I blushed when I realized he and Riley had seen the whole thing. "You were right," he said to Riley, next. "She couldn't do it."

Riley looked embarrassed, like she hadn't wanted Evan to say what he'd said in front of me, and I stiffened and turned away from her. It felt like she was taunting me. There she was, with a boyfriend who adored her, and she was openly telling that boyfriend that there was no way I could muster up the courage to even talk to an older guy.

I sat outside with them in silence for a few minutes, mindlessly taking sips of my drink, until suddenly it was gone and I had to go to the bathroom. "Be right back," I told them, and wandered inside, teetering slightly and trying to shake off a little dizziness.

Grace and her more-than-a-friend were the only ones inside when I got there, and they were sitting on the couch in the living room together now, talking in whispers and hisses in a tone that I instinctively knew meant they were fighting, even despite the fact that I was a little drunk and my perceptiveness was suffering.

I slipped inside the bathroom in the hallway as quietly as I could and dabbed at my face with a wet washcloth when I was done, hoping it would cool me off. My face felt hot, and I knew it was probably from the alcohol.

When I left the bathroom, Grace was waiting outside alone. "Oh, sorry," I mumbled. "If I had known someone was waiting..."

"Don't worry about it. I'm just getting some water. Nicole said the kitchen sink only has hot right now until someone can come to fix it." She showed me the glass in her hand, and I nodded my understanding as I got out of her way. She didn't close the doorway behind herself, so I lingered in the hallway when I realized the other girl had gone back outside.

"Was that girl your girlfriend?" I asked her. She let out

a light laugh as she filled the glass, and I had to wait a few seconds for her answer while she took several gulps of water.

"Um, no. It's a little bit more complicated than that. You wouldn't get it."

I furrowed my eyebrows, uncertain if her offending me had been intentional. "I'm not twelve, you know. I'm seventeen."

"Ah. Right. Super mature," she joked. Her smile faded when she saw I was glaring. "I'm kidding! Kind of." She set the glass aside and told me, "Alright, so I'm feeling charitable tonight. I'm gonna give you some advice for college. You ready?"

"Okay," I replied, eager to hear what she had to say. "Ready."

"Before you ever even flirt with a girl... or guy, in your case... make sure you both have the same intentions. Especially if it's someone you're friends with. Because if one of you wants to hook up and one of you wants more, it gets really complicated really quickly. And you do *not* want complicated if you were going for casual."

"So she likes you more than you like her," I realized. "That's not the worst problem in the world to have."

"Yeah, I guess not, but..." She picked up the glass again, took a drink, and then set it back down on the bathroom counter. "She got all of the shallow stuff out back in high school, so now she wants to get serious with someone. I didn't get the opportunity to have a few shallow relationships back then, so I'd like to have some fun first. Maybe in a couple of years I'll date." She paused, then laughed again. "I can't believe I'm having this conversation with Nicole's kid sister."

"I'm not a kid," I repeated. "I've dated around more than you have, probably."

"Ouch," she laughed. "But you kind of have the advantage of liking guys. I saw you eyeing Michael, by the way. He has a girlfriend."

"I wasn't eyeing him," I denied. "And even if I had been, I wouldn't want to date him."

"Sure," she said in a way that told me she didn't believe me. I grit my teeth, frustrated.

"I'm serious. I broke up with my boyfriend in March. I just want something with no pressure and no feelings. That way I won't get hurt again."

"That's... kind of sad," Grace replied, folding her arms across her chest. She looked like she felt sorry for me for a moment, but then that disappeared and she let out a dramatic sigh. "Well, if only you were about two years older, were into girls, and weren't my roommate's little sister. Maybe in another life, huh?"

She straightened up, like she was about to leave, and I blurted out, unthinkingly, "I could like girls. You don't know."

She arched an eyebrow at me. "You? Uh huh, sure. Look, there's a baby lesbian at this party, but it isn't you, honey."

"I'm serious," I pressed, only half-registering what she'd said. I wasn't even sure why I was arguing with her; the goal had been to find a guy to help distract myself with. Not a girl who'd just exacerbate the problem. But being brushed off wasn't something I handled well, and not being taken seriously was something I handled even worse. "I've thought about kissing girls before."

She raised a hand to smother a laugh. "Oh... I don't even know what to say to that, honestly. Um. Are you propositioning me?"

"No. I don't know." I bit my lip and blinked until my vision was clearer.

"I've got a feeling there's a lot of stuff you don't know." She sighed and moved to leave the bathroom. "Anyway, this has definitely been the highlight of my night, but for both of our sakes, I promise I won't tell Nicole about this. Talk to you later?"

She paused, and it seemed to dawn on her that I was a little intoxicated and that she was supposed to be watching me for my sister. She turned to me, waiting for confirmation, and I glanced away from her, blinking back tears as I leaned against the wall and stared at my feet. I felt humiliated, and I couldn't even pinpoint why.

"Whoa, hey," said Grace, rejoining me. "Don't cry. I didn't mean to upset you. I thought you were kidding. If you're having serious feelings about girls, we can... I don't know, talk about it? If you wanted." She glanced down the hallway, presumably to make sure no one else was around, and then seemed frustrated when I didn't say anything to her. "Is there something I can do...?"

I glanced to her, too confused about what I actually wanted to even begin to answer her question. She wasn't much taller than me already, and she was leaning over, her hand pressed to the wall at my head, so we were at each other's eye level. She took one look at me and practically groaned. "You look like a lost puppy. There's no way you're guilting me into this, you know."

"Into what?" I mumbled, but I knew that she'd noticed how close we were right around the same time that I had. She shot me an exasperated look, and I felt the corners of my lips turn upwards against my will. Mostly because of the look on her face: like someone had just told her an injured animal had been left on her doorstep and needed to be taken care of and she *really* didn't want to do it even though deep down she knew she was going to.

She visibly bit back a smile of her own, shook her head one short time, and then told me, "Once, and you *never* tell your sister, alright?"

I swallowed hard and hid my surprise, though I imagined it wasn't well, given that my brain still wasn't functioning at one hundred percent. Still, Grace was pretty, and I *was* a little curious, and I knew it wouldn't mean anything, so I nodded at her and then waited, resting the back of my head against the wall.

She glanced down the hallway again, and when she didn't see or hear anyone coming, she moved in closer to me and then paused, like she was collecting herself. I watched her with a lump in my throat and my heart pounding in my chest. Some parts of me felt like they were trembling and others felt like they were made of jelly. I'd worked myself up into a panic in a matter of seconds and I didn't know what the hell I was doing. I thought briefly about stopping her before I decided against it.

Grace rested one hand on my neck and moved in toward me. I felt her chest and stomach against mine and didn't dare move an inch, and when her nose brushed mine, I closed my eyes and held my breath, determined to stay completely still for a reason I didn't really understand. I pressed both of my palms to the wall behind me.

Her lips were soft and gentle and she kissed slowly, like she knew – and she *did* know – that I'd never kissed a girl before. She tasted like strawberries, kind of, and I knew that was from the fruity mixed drinks some of the older kids had been drinking earlier. I decided I'd try one when I got back outside. It tasted good.

When she kissed me harder, my hands came off the wall, and I moved them to her hips, resting them there with a very light, uncertain touch. I felt her smile when I did that, and she mumbled something into my mouth that sounded kind of like "cute" right before she nipped at my lip and then used her free hand to press one of my hands down harder against her hip. I found one of the belt loops of her jeans with my other hand and used it to gently tug her closer.

Kissing Grace was kind of like kissing a guy, in that she led the whole thing and I kind of just went along with it, partially because I was frozen with anxiety and also because I was worried I was somehow bad at it given my inexperience with kissing girls. But it was also different in a lot of ways. I noticed that she kissed softer than any guy I'd ever been with and that she smelled nicer. So with her leading our kiss, it was kind of like being pressed to the wall by a sweet-smelling pillow as opposed to feeling stuck between a hard wall I was attracted to and a hard wall that was actually just a wall.

She also didn't shove her tongue down my throat, which was nice. That part – the tongue part – was my favorite difference.

Right around the time I was able to draw *that* comparison – when it was just starting to get really good, in other words – was when Evan squeaked out, "Kayla?" from down the hallway. Grace detached herself from me before he could even get my full name out, and I turned my head so quickly my neck gave a painful throb.

He blinked at us, wide-eyed, and then glanced back the way he'd just come, like he couldn't process the series of events that had led to him standing right where he was at that very moment. "What are you doing?" he asked me once he'd picked his jaw up off of the floor.

It was apparent that Grace was going to let me handle this, so I fumbled my words for a moment before I finally got out, "Really drunk." It seemed like the best excuse to go with given the circumstances, and, in all fairness, it was about half-true. I was drunk enough to do something I'd have never done sober, but sober enough that I'd been able to *not* do if I really hadn't wanted to.

"What the hell is wrong with you?"

I opened my mouth to respond, but then I realized that this question had been directed to Grace.

"Me? It's a party; lighten up." Grace rolled her eyes at him even as she walked down the hallway and brushed by him. "Everyone does stupid stuff when they're drunk. Get used to it."

She disappeared outside, and I let out a small sigh of relief, satisfied with her answer. "You okay?" Evan asked me, suddenly beside me, and I nodded at him, unable to look him directly in the eyes. I was worried he'd somehow realize how heavy my eyelids felt as an after-effect of a very good make out session with Grace, or that he'd see something else in my expression that gave away how I really felt about what I'd just done.

"Please don't tell Riley," I murmured to him, and though he seemed hesitant at first, he nodded and took my hand to help walk me back outside.

"I won't. But you should seriously tell your sister her friend's a creep."

"Maybe," I said, and then, a beat later, added, "Thanks for saving me." I felt something sink in my chest and regretted saying it.

"Any time," he replied, tightening his grip on me as we descended down the front porch steps, and my guilt only worsened from there.

***

The rest of that night was a massive blur of not being able to look anyone in the eyes. Not Grace, who seemed just as content with ignoring me as I was to ignore her. Not Nicole, who wouldn't have known whether to kill me or Grace first if she'd found out what we'd done. Not Evan, who very quickly got nearly as drunk as I was and then turned red any time we made eye contact. And *certainly* not Riley, who I was paranoid would notice I was acting weirdly and confront me at any moment.

But that didn't happen. Riley was kind of sullen and withdrawn for the remainder of the party. Had I not had my own issues to deal with, I'd probably have asked her if something had happened to upset her. But as it was, I was a little distracted.

I passed out quickly in my bed once the party was over, and woke up in the afternoon to the sound of my phone buzzing. Someone was calling me.

In the ten seconds or so it took me to roll over and retrieve my phone from my nightstand, I relived the events of the previous night and was struck with mild horror. When I saw that the person calling me was Evan, the horror turned to panic. I immediately rejected the call. I wasn't ready to defend myself to him.

And what could I say, other than "I was just drunk"? I couldn't tell him that I'd been the one to come on to Grace. I couldn't tell him that I'd only come on to Grace in the first place because I'd come to the realization that I was a little bicurious. Because if I told him those things, he'd wonder *how* I'd come to that realization, and I'd have to tell him that it'd involved Riley cuddling with me in my bed like we had hundreds of other times and probably would hundreds of *more* times provided I kept my mouth shut.

I sucked in another sharp breath as my phone rang again. It was Evan. He really wasn't going to let this go.

I pressed the green button and raised the phone to my

ear to croak out, "Hello?"

"Kayla." He seemed relieved, not confrontational, which was a pleasant surprise. "You're alive."

"You woke me up," I told him, unamused.

"Oh. I'm sorry. It's two o'clock. I thought you were just avoiding me." I didn't answer him, and after a pause, he asked me, "Are you okay?"

"I'm fine," I said. "Just kind of have a hangover."

"Yeah. Last night got kind of... weird."

"I guess." I tried to sound casual. "It wasn't that weird."

"I'd say it was pretty strange. You, uh... you *do* remember what happened, right?"

"Yes, Evan." I heaved an audible sigh. I knew how I needed to play this. He was the weird one for making it into a big deal. *Obviously* it hadn't meant anything. Girls kissed at parties all the time. Throw in a little "I drank a lot" and I was in the clear. "It's not a big deal," I told him.

"I-" he started, and then paused, sounding confused. "It wasn't a peck, Kayla, c'mon."

"I had a lot to drink," I argued. "I guess I get kind of promiscuous when I drink too much. At least now I know. I have this theory that Riley's a sad drunk. That would explain last night, anyway. What was up with her?"

"What was up with *you*?" Evan countered, refusing to change the subject. I held back another sigh. "That wasn't a cute party kiss, Kayla. She might've started it, and you've might've been drunk, but you guys were really going at it. She had her tongue in your mouth."

103

"Why do you care so much about who I kiss?" I snapped.

"Because I'm your friend!" he shot back. "You've been going through some stuff, and I know I haven't been the best friend to you these past couple of months, but I want to be. You lost Josh, and I guess maybe it feels like you've lost a part of Riley and me, too. But you don't have to do stuff like this; this self-destructive crap reads like a massive cry for help. You don't get to do this stuff and then ignore the people answering the cry."

"You're so smart, Evan," I sighed out. "Is that what you want me to tell you? That you've got me all figured out? Maybe I'm allowed to have fun with people that aren't you or Riley. Wasn't that what you said? That I deserve to have a little fun?"

"You know what I meant by that. I thought you were going to go flirt with that guy. Maybe get his number. Not french some chick you just met! And you thanked me last night. You said I saved you from her. I know you regretted kissing her, so you don't get to act like it was some casual fun thing you wanted to do. You lost control."

"Well, it's time for me to take some of it back, then," I said. "Why I don't I start with ending this phone call?"

"Don't-" he began, but I ended the call with a jab from my thumb and then turned my phone off.

I wondered, for a moment, if he was going to tell Riley what had happened. Then I decided I didn't care.

If she found out, I'd lie to her, same as I'd lied to him. I'd lie to everyone, if that was what it took to avoid making this into a big deal.

I'd even lie to myself.

Chapter Six

It became clear the next time I finally got around to spending time with Riley and Evan again that Evan and I had a silent understanding: if I didn't mention the night of Nicole's party, he wouldn't mention it, either. Riley remained clueless, and it made it easier for us to keep hanging out like nothing had changed.

I noticed that the party *had*, in fact, affected our group when we all went swimming at the pool again. This time, we went at night, when it was deserted and the water was warm. I laid down in one of the recliners to relax while Riley stripped down to her bikini beside me, and I glanced first to her, very determined to keep it to *just* a glance, and then to Evan, who was a few feet away, watching the both of us carefully as he took his shoes off.

When she was finished, Riley turned to me and sat down on the end of my recliner. "You should get in," she told me, placing a hand on my thigh. "I'm gonna need the extra firepower on my side if Evan and I get into a splash-off."

My face warmed as she leaned toward me slightly, increasing the weight on her hand. "Go without me," I told her. "I'll get in later."

"You sure?"

Evan joined us before I could reply. "Riley, c'mon. The water's warm; it's nice." He pulled her to her feet and I watched him steer her away, a possessive arm around her waist. My eyebrows furrowed.

"Hey! Actually, I think I *will* get in," I decided, and got to my feet. Riley beamed at me and rushed from Evan to grab at my hand. I noticed Evan watching us with a frustrated look on his face, but I dismissed him to grin back at Riley as she tugged me to the water's edge. Together, we leapt in.

Evan joined us once we'd resurfaced, and we all treaded water for a moment, adjusting to the temperature.

"I'm glad we can all still hang out and it's not weird," Riley admitted. "It was touch and go for a while there."

"I don't know; it's not totally the same." Evan looked over at me and his eyes narrowed slightly. "There have definitely been some weird changes."

"We agree there," I replied stiffly, meeting him head-on with my own stare.

Riley looked back and forth between us for a moment,

clearly confused. "Okay... *anyway*, I was thinking we could play Sharks and Minnows. You guys up for it?"

"Maybe," Evan said non-committedly. "I might just swim around for a little bit. And I really have to pee."

"Then why'd you get in?" Riley asked him. "Go to the bathroom."

"You guys were getting in; I wanted to get in, too," he argued, embarrassed. "What are you going to do while I'm gone?"

"Uh... wait for you to get back?" asked Riley. "Can you please just go before you pee in the pool?" She shot him a strange look and then turned to look at me as though to ask, "*What's up with him?*" Evan noticed and went red.

"Okay, fine. I'll be right back." He lifted himself out of the pool and then walked away, but not before glancing over his shoulder at us just before he rounded the corner to head into the men's room.

"What was that?" Riley asked me almost instantly, drifting toward the wall and then pressing her back against it. Her arms came up out of the water and she gripped at the edge of the pool with both hands.

I shrugged my shoulders, more than willing to ignore whatever was up with Evan for as long as I could. If he wanted to be weird about what'd happened at Nicole's party, then that was fine with me. I'd just refuse to acknowledge his weirdness – and the oddly possessive behavior that had seemed to come with it – until he finally got over it.

"I feel like you two are exchanging looks every time

you think I'm not paying attention," Riley told me, arching an eyebrow. "For like the past few days, anyway. You two aren't into each other, too, are you?" She grinned to let me know she was joking, but I knew without asking that she was still curious about what was up with us.

"You caught us," I deflected, giving an overdramatic sigh.

"The real reason you're against us dating comes out," Riley played along, grinning.

"I'm not against it," I lied. "I just didn't expect it."

"You know that I didn't expect it to happen either," Riley admitted. "But don't tell Evan that."

"Must have been a shock when he kissed you." I was growing tired of treading water, so I swam over to join Riley against the wall, watching her carefully for a reaction.

"Yeah." She gave a laugh I could tell she had to force out, and her smile was small and thoughtful. "He caught me off guard, that's for sure."

We fell silent for a moment, just enjoying each other's company, and I adjusted myself a little, moving so that I could stretch out, let go of the wall, and float. I tilted my head back and closed my eyes, drifting in the gentle water. I thought of Prom night: the last night things had been normal. The night I'd spent an hour in my bathroom with Riley, turning her into someone beautiful enough for me to notice.

Evan had always noticed her.

A small fountain of water landed on my cheek and

splashed across my face, and I floundered, struggling to right myself as Riley laughed at me. When I twisted around to face her, she was sinking down into the pool to gather another mouthful of water. I gaped at her. "Did you just spit on me?"

She nodded, grinning, as she rose back up, mouth full and ready to fire.

"No!" I screeched, darting toward her in an effort to keep her from gathering fresh ammo after she inevitably released a second mouthful. This time she caught me on the shoulder just before I pinned her to the wall, my hands gripping the concrete on either side of her as she threw her head back and laughed so loudly that I was sure Evan could hear her from the bathroom.

That reminded me that he'd been gone for at least a minute now, and I looked over my shoulder, curious. "What's taking him so long?"

When I looked back to Riley, her mouth was open like she'd been about to reply, but she closed it the instant we locked eyes. We were very close. Way *too* close, actually. Her arms had reentered the pool at some point, and I could feel water rushing past my legs beneath us as she kicked back and forth with her legs to stay afloat.

"I... um," Riley tried to say, and I saw her eyes dart to my lips even as I pushed off of the wall and moved away from her. My face was red, I knew, but hers was even redder, and that was what really scared me.

I twisted around and swam away, and when Riley uncertainly called out my name, I sucked in a breath and then dipped beneath the water, swimming along the floor of the pool with my eyes open and focused on the wall at the other end. It wasn't long before my lungs began to burn, but I propelled myself forward a few feet at a time, trying not to expend any more energy than I had to. My urge to avoid Riley was greater than my need for air, and besides, burning lungs hurt less than the searing feeling in my chest that'd never quite gone away.

I reached out and touched the wall as I reached the other side, then opened my mouth and let the air rush out in the form of a stream of bubbles as I pushed off the floor and broke through the surface. I sucked in air, panting hard, and reached up to run my hands over my head, getting my hair out of my face.

When I finally gathered the courage to turn back to look across the pool at Riley, I was relieved to see that Evan had rejoined her and was lowering himself into the pool. He was saying something to her that I couldn't quite hear, but her eyes were still on me, and she was chewing at her lip with a worried look on her face.

I turned away and slowly made my way over to the stairs in the shallow end, then straightened my bathing suit as I climbed out of the pool. From there, I headed to where I'd left my flip-flops and towel. "I'm gonna head home," I told Evan and Riley. "You guys should have some alone time."

"Okay," said Evan at the same time that Riley asked, "What?" They looked at each other, and then Evan shot her a strange look before twisting around in the pool to face me.

"We'll see you around, Kayla." He wasn't even trying

to hide that he was more than willing to get rid of me, and Riley picked up on it, too. I could tell from just one glance in her direction that while she may not have been sure about what was going on, she definitely didn't like Evan's tone.

"Kayla, you don't have to go," she said, but I didn't even look at her. To Evan, she added, "Look, I don't know why you guys are acting weird all of a sudden, but you need to sort it out."

"Why is it my fault?" Evan asked, defensive. "You should ask *Kayla* what's going on with her."

"Evan," I snapped at him in warning, but he gave me a look and shrugged his shoulders.

"I'm just saying. Maybe Riley would be helpful, since you won't hear anything I have to say."

I shook my head at him, glaring, and then wrapped my towel around myself and stormed out of the pool area. Riley called out, "Kayla!" like she could tell that I was leaving because of her and not Evan, but I only upped my pace, refusing to look back.

***

Nicole was up watching a movie in the living room by the time I got back, and I changed into my pajamas and joined her, plopping down next to her and stealing a handful of popcorn from the bowl in her lap. She acknowledged me with a glance and a soft smile.

"Have fun?"

"Tons," I deadpanned, regretting joining her when I

felt tears prick at the corners of my eyes. I didn't know what to think or what to feel anymore. As much as I didn't want to believe it, I was pretty sure that Evan was being so possessive of Riley again because he was worried that I liked girls, and I was also pretty sure that whatever I'd felt with Riley in the pool had at least been partially mutual. But the idea of acknowledging that I'd felt something was about as palatable as slicing off one of my toes. Evan and Riley were complicated enough. The last thing I needed in my life was to be part of a love triangle.

"I think it's just puppy love. It'll fade," Nicole advised me, and it took me a moment to realize she was talking about Evan and Riley. "We both remember *our* first big crushes. You clearer than me, given that yours is fresher." She smirked at me. "The butterflies, the tingling, the little gasp-y feeling you get when you first see him. I'd have done anything just to see Cody Juergens smile at me. I was obsessed with him for six months before we finally dated. I mean, it was ninth grade, but still."

I sat in silence, knees pulled up to my chest and my head tilted back to rest against the couch cushion behind me. I stared at our ceiling as the light from the TV tinted it different colors, trying to remember how I'd felt about Josh my sophomore year. What Nicole had said rang true. The butterflies, the tingles... it'd all been there. I'd been sure before that I'd been in love, but now I wasn't as confident.

"Have you ever been in love?" I asked her. "Like, real

love?"

"Not unless you think that what I felt in ninth grade was love," said Nicole with a laugh. "Because that's about as good as it's gotten for me."

"Something tells me that's not real love," I decided. "I don't think that's how it feels. Maybe at first, I guess, but not once you've really gotten there and you're *actually* in love."

"Hmm." Nicole tossed a piece of popcorn into her mouth and asked, non-committedly, "What do you think it feels like, then?"

"Not sure." I paused and closed my eyes. I could remember feeling butterflies with Josh early on, and for a long time afterward. Maybe they'd never really faded. Maybe *that* was because I'd never truly grown accustomed to being with him. Even when we'd broken up, he'd still felt new and unfamiliar.

But he hadn't been the first person I'd felt butterflies for. He hadn't been the first person I'd seen and immediately knew I wanted to be around.

I remembered, with a sudden jolt to my chest, that that'd happened in first grade, and that just a few short minutes later, I'd walked right up to Riley and declared that she was going to be my best friend.

"Maybe you're right, though," mused Nicole, pulling me out of my head. "Eventually it must just feel... comfortable. Or, like... warm." She gave a short laugh. "Maybe love is like eating a microwaved slice of chocolate cake. With hot fudge sauce poured onto it." She paused. "Now I really want cake."

"Bet you still have some left over from your party," I mumbled, still perturbed by my thoughts.

"I do. Thanks for the reminder." She patted my knee once, gratefully, and then stood to head into the kitchen.

By the time she'd returned, I was upstairs in bed, more confused than ever and with zero chance of getting any sleep.

**

Putting my phone on silent shortly after leaving the pool turned out to be an excellent idea, because I was able to wait until morning to face what I expected to be an inevitable barrage of texts.

Except I didn't have a million missed texts, actually. There were just a couple from Riley. The first said: *"Evan told me about what happened. We need to talk."* The second, sent an hour after the first, said: *"Talk to me. Please?"*

I left my phone on my nightstand and went downstairs to eat breakfast. It was a Sunday, so Mom and Nicole were in the kitchen when I got there, Mom standing by the counter eating an English muffin while Nicole texted someone at the table, a bagel on a plate in front of her. I stole half of it from her and took a bite.

"Hey!" She snatched it back, and I scowled at her, then went to the fridge to scavenge for something to eat.

"Any plans for the day?" Mom asked me. "Nicole and I were thinking about renting some movies. It's supposed to rain today. I have to run to the store so I was thinking about picking a couple up on the way home."

"I guess," I said, shrugging.

"Do you have any you'd like to see?"

"No. I'll just watch whatever you two want." I found an uneaten cheese stick and then closed the fridge.

"Are you okay, honey?" Mom asked me. I turned to see both her and Nicole watching me, and wondered if I really looked as miserable as I felt. I forced myself to perk up and offered them a smile.

"Sorry... just didn't get much sleep. I might go take a nap."

"Want us to come get you when we're ready to watch?" Mom asked, though she still looked concerned.

I nodded. "Yeah, just wake me up." When they still stared at me, I asked, "What? I'm fine. Just tired. Seriously."

"You haven't been the same since you and Josh ended things," Mom mentioned tentatively, like she'd been trying to decide for a while when the best time to bring this up was.

"I'm fine," I insisted, more forcefully this time. Mom looked away from me and pressed her lips into a thin line. It was a look that said she'd expected me to react exactly how I was reacting. I softened and let out a sigh. "I really am. I'm just *tired*. I'll come watch movies later, I swear."

"You can talk to me, honey. You know that, right?"

"And me," Nicole added.

"I know. There's just... nothing to talk about." I took the cheese stick with me and left the kitchen, but threw it in the garbage the instant I was out of sight, suddenly not very hungry anymore.

Chapter Seven

The whole "living in the same neighborhood with Riley and Evan" thing worked both ways. I could find Riley when she didn't want to be found. But she could find *me* when I didn't want to be found, either.

She knocked this time. Not on the front door, but on my bedroom door. I thought it was Mom, asking me to watch a movie, until I heard her voice, gentle and anxious. "Kayla?"

I let out a sigh and sat up, pulling out the ear bud I had in one of my ears. The other was already out, resting on my bed so that I could hear my Mom when she came to get me. I wished I'd put it in, now, on the off chance that not responding would've just made Riley leave.

That turned out not to be the case, anyway, because after about ten seconds of me staring silently at my closed door, the knob turned and it cracked open to comically reveal just one of Riley's eyes. I'd have laughed if I'd been in a better mood.

"Can I come in?" she asked.

I grimaced. "Does my answer make a difference?"

She hesitated, pondering my question for a moment. "Honestly, I don't know. I'd rather not have to figure it out."

I closed my eyes and let out a silent breath, certain I'd regret letting her in. "Come in," I said.

She slid inside and closed the door behind herself, then stared at me for several seconds, her back pressed to the door and her teeth worrying her bottom lip. I glanced up at her and then down to my cross-legged lap, over and over again, until she finally spoke.

"You didn't tell me."

She sounded hurt, which surprised me for some reason. I'd almost expected her to treat my kiss with Grace like some shocking piece of gossip, which I realized now was totally unlike Riley and much more like a reaction Vanessa would've had. Riley's primary concern, as always, was us. Our friendship, our trust in each other, our closeness.

I put myself into her shoes for a moment and realized that a part of her was probably scared. I'd hid something big from her, and I'd never done that before. We'd been spending less time together, and we hadn't been quite as close, and she'd worked hard to make sure we wouldn't grow apart because of her relationship with Evan, but now here we were. To her, it was probably the most concrete evidence she had that I was pulling away from her.

And I was. But I was sure she didn't know the entire reason why, because I'd yet to completely work it out myself.

"I didn't tell anyone," I said at last. "Evan saw."

She hesitated, and then crossed the room to join me on my bed, facing me with one leg bent at the knee and folded under her while the other hung off of the edge of the bed. I knew she was looking at me, so I glued my gaze to a spot on my right ankle and didn't look up.

"I still wish you'd told me," she said.

"It wasn't a big deal," I mumbled. "It didn't mean anything."

There was a long silence as the half-lie hung in the air, and Riley reached out and took my hand. I knew immediately that she didn't believe me.

"Hey," she murmured, and I squeezed her hand hard, my vision growing bleary as my eyes fogged over and my throat tightened. I wouldn't look at her. I couldn't.

"I'm scared," I admitted at last, and felt Riley squeeze my hand back. "I don't know what's happening to me. I don't know what I..." I sucked in a breath and amended, "If I even like..."

I stopped there. I couldn't say it aloud.

"That's okay," Riley breathed out, but I could feel her trembling slightly across from me. My heart pounded in my chest and I looked up at last.

Riley's eyes were shiny, like she wanted to cry too, and I was confused when I saw that. She was my best friend, and I knew that she hurt when I hurt, but this seemed more intimate than that.

"I'm sorry," she said. "I was so..." She seemed to struggle with how to finish her sentence. "So... caught up in juggling my own mess and the little bit of yours that I could see, with all of the drama with Evan and me and then you feeling left out. And I asked you if that was all that was wrong just to make sure, because I wondered if..." She hesitated, and then never finished that thought. "I just didn't actually look hard enough to see if I was missing something."

She swallowed hard and raised her free hand to my cheek to wipe away a tear with her thumb, continuing, "And I hate that I missed this. I am the *last* person that should've missed this." Her voice shook for her last sentence, and her hand lingered, her thumb brushing gently along my cheek. "Because I guess a selfish part of me was looking for it."

I opened my mouth but found myself at a loss for words, my eyes still glued to hers. Something passed between us, and I knew right then that I wanted to kiss her. I knew a lot of things right then. Why Riley'd always taken my hand at every opportunity and why she'd always laughed at even the dumbest of my jokes. Why she'd never had a boyfriend, and why she'd only gotten one after I'd made it completely clear that I supported the idea. Why the most affection I'd ever seen her give Evan was a kiss on the cheek. Why she'd kissed him on Prom night, while I was supposed to have been off losing my virginity Josh. Why she'd disliked Josh much more than Evan ever had.

"Oh," I whispered, stunned. I let go of her hand, which very clearly caught her off-guard, and said, "Evan. You used him." I looked up at her, eyebrows furrowed and heart in my stomach. "How could you use him?"

"I... I didn't-" she stuttered. I could tell my reaction had surprised her. Knowing we had feelings for each other was supposed to be the big shocker, but I'd been processing that possibility since our moment in the pool the previous night. Riley using Evan, however, was out of left field. "I didn't mean to," she said at last. "He's my best friend, so I thought... I was sure you'd never– and I thought that maybe he would be different, because he's my best friend and I love him."

I just stared at her, my mouth very quickly going dry. I could tell she was panicking, as though the full weight of what she'd done was finally crashing down onto her.

"I thought I was doing the right thing," she squeaked out. "I thought you'd never– You were with Josh, and I thought maybe it wasn't girls, it was that you were my friend. And *he* was my friend, too, and he liked me."

"Oh," I breathed out, feeling slightly sick. "Oh, I can't do this." I stood up and ran a hand through my hair, then began to pace back and forth while Riley watched me from the bed. "I don't even know what I *am*, Riley! I can't deal with this, too."

"I screwed up, I know," she pressed, getting to her feet, too. When I didn't stop moving, she grabbed at my hand and spun me to face her. "Kayla, calm down."

"How am I supposed to calm down?" I blurted out. "I

don't know why I feel this way, or *when* I started to feel this way, or… if I'm even *allowed* to feel this way. He's our best friend, and you're…" I tried to force the word out, but in my panic, it caught in my throat. Riley bit her lip so hard it turned white as she watched me. At last, I managed to say it. "You're… *gay*. He's head over heels for you and you're gay."

She exhaled sharply, her eyes on mine. She didn't argue with me. She just said, "I thought there was a chance I wasn't."

"*I* can't be," I insisted, letting her go and taking a step back. "I like boys."

"Maybe you like both," said Riley very quietly, as though she didn't want to offend me with the idea.

I wasn't offended, but I still didn't want to hear it. Entertaining the idea of being gay was much easier, because I could tell myself I wasn't until I was blue in the face and my arguments made sense. Trying to convince myself I wasn't bisexual sounded a lot harder.

But whatever I was, there was no denying that I was attracted to Riley. And I had absolutely no idea how I was supposed to handle that.

"You should go," I told her, "and we should pretend that this never happened."

"I can't do that," was her immediate reply. "And even if I did, it's not like we could just forget."

"We could try."

"I don't want to try," insisted Riley.

"Then just go!" I snapped, sure I was about to burst into tears. I couldn't process so much information in such a short amount of time. My world was turned on its head. I liked Riley, and Riley liked me back, and she was dating the absolute *worst* person she could be, given the circumstances.

"Calm down," whispered Riley, giving my bedroom door a nervous glance.

"Why should I?" I shot back. "You knew how you felt and you dated Evan anyway. How could you do that to him?"

At that, Riley straightened up, angry. "You lied about being okay with it, remember? You told me you wanted me to go for it, and given the conversation we're having right now, I think it's safe to say you were *never* okay with it."

"I didn't know what you knew," I insisted. "I didn't know that I felt..." Frustrated, I gestured back and forth between us. "*This!* I think it would've been a little bit of a stretch to predict this way back on Prom night."

"Exactly. I thought that if I was ever going to love a guy, it'd be Evan, and you were with Josh when I kissed him. And when you told me you wanted me to say yes to Evan, I did. By the time I knew I didn't feel that way about him, it seemed better to just let him be happy, because it wasn't like I was going to get to be with the person I wanted to be with anyway." She let out a sigh and reached up to rub at her temples. "Can we just... stop blaming each other, and just figure out how we're going to deal with this and what we're going to do?"

"You can't date him anymore," I pointed out. "And you can't break his heart."

"Unfortunately, those two things are mutually exclusive."

"Well... then..." I paused and folded my arms across my chest, chewing on the inside of my cheek. "I don't know. It's not right to keep leading him on, Riley. It's not fair to him or to you. But... I'm confused, okay? I don't want you to think that just because you end things with him..." I trailed off, hoping she'd understand, and the saddened look she gave me told me she did. "I just need to figure things out," I insisted.

There was a long silence, and then Riley took a deep breath. "I'm gonna go," she told me. "Okay?"

"Are you mad?" I asked her nervously.

She shook her head. "No. How can I-" She paused, and then amended, "I'm just not mad. I actually, um... this kind of feels like a dream. And I just need to think. Away from you." She reached out to touch my hand with hers, and then turned to leave my room. "I'll, um... I'll call you later? Or I'll come over. I don't know which yet. Or when."

"Okay," I managed to get out, and then she was gone and the door was closed behind her. I blinked rapidly, trying to absorb what'd just transpired between us.

As it all began to sink in, my brain finally managed to simplify what felt like a very complicated situation: Evan loved Riley. Riley loved me. And I...

Well, I was very, *very* confused.

***

125

Mom waited until our second movie was over and Nicole had announced that she was going to go watch Netflix on her laptop before she brought up Riley. As much as I'd hoped she'd forget to mention it, I realized that Riley had probably not been able to hide how upset she'd been when she'd left, and not much got past my mother when she was truly paying attention.

"So Riley didn't stay for long today," was her opening line. She shifted next to me on the couch, facing me with her back against the armrest. The empty popcorn bowl rested between us as she asked, "Did you two have a fight?"

"No, Mom," I sighed out. "We're fine."

"She looked pretty upset." Mom paused, then shot me a knowing look. "Oh. Did she and Evan break up?"

"No," I repeated, but I was intrigued by the question. "Why would you think they broke up?"

"Well..." Mom hesitated, and I raised both eyebrows, silently urging her to keep going. "I'd appreciate it if you didn't repeat this to either of them, because I wouldn't want to hurt their feelings, but I always thought it was a little strange that the two of them were dating."

"Why?" I sat up straighter, growing even more curious. Had my mom seen something even I'd been blind to? She'd watched the three of us grow up, after all.

My insides went icy for a moment when I wondered if maybe she'd guessed that there was something between Riley and me. I had no clue how she'd react to me even kissing a girl, let alone dating one, and I wasn't eager to find out.

"Well, you and Riley were much closer to each other than you were to Evan growing up," Mom told me, and I felt my heart begin to beat faster. "Which is typical of young girls, obviously. But he used to trail after the two of you like a lost puppy. It was very cute, but it was also very clear that neither of you were interested. And this is getting into your middle school years, too. I do recall him being very enamored with Riley, then, but never the other way around." She looked thoughtful. "Things change once you reach dating age, though, I suppose. Sometimes the people you least expect make the best couples."

"Yeah," I echoed, unable to look her in the eyes. "I guess they do."

***

My doorbell rang the following day, and I answered with butterflies in my stomach, certain it was going to be Riley.

It wasn't. Instead, it was Evan.

He offered me a nervous smile and held up an eight-pack of Coke, my favorite soda. "Peace offering."

"You didn't have to," I told him. Just the sight of him made me feel guilty.

"I wanted to. I know it seems like every other week we have issues, but I mean it this time. I'm turning over a new leaf. I guess... honestly, seeing you with Grace just freaked me out."

"Oh." I stood in the doorway for a long moment, and then realized it'd be rude not to invite him in. I opened the door wider and he nodded thankfully, stepping inside and giving me room to close the door behind him.

In the hand that wasn't carrying the soda, he held what I assumed was a DVD case until he showed it to me. "It's a computer game that just came out last year," he explained. "I know you don't love video games, but this one doesn't involve a lot of skill. It's more about exploring the world, and the graphics are really cool. I thought I'd show it to you. The installation shouldn't take long, and I'll demonstrate it if you want."

"That sounds like a great idea," I agreed, offering him a smile. He grinned back at me, relieved.

"Awesome."

We went upstairs to my room together and, much to my disappointment, he continued the conversation we'd been having while he'd been outside. As he slid the CD into my laptop's disk drive while we sat together on my bed, he told me, "Anyway, I guess if I'm being totally honest... The thing is, you and Riley have always been really close. I always felt a little left out growing up. Up until maybe seventh or eighth grade. And even though we all don't get a chance to hang out as much as we used to, you guys are *still* really close. Combine that, me being a paranoid ass, and you kissing another girl... and I kind of... like I said: freaked. But I know I was wrong now."

"Oh," I said again. I knew that he was, in a roundabout way, trying to tell me that he was paranoid about me having feelings for Riley. He wasn't wrong, and

128

I couldn't bring myself to tell him that he was when it wasn't the truth.

He was being sweeter to me than I deserved, and even tried to change the subject once it was clear he'd explained himself well enough. "Speaking of Riley, have you heard from her? I didn't talk to her at all yesterday, actually. She said she was going to talk to you and then never answered my text." He shot me a nervous look. "You guys are okay, right?"

"Yeah," I forced myself to say. "We're fine. Everything's all cleared up."

"Good. I figured I'd leave you guys a day or two to deal with the drama. I felt really bad once I got over being... paranoid, and all. It wasn't my secret to tell. I was just trying to help. It felt like you lost your way for a bit there, and I thought maybe Riley was the best person to, you know, slap you out of it or whatever."

"It's okay, Evan," I insisted. "Really. Don't feel bad. About anything."

"Well, I do. But I'm glad I'm forgiven. You can keep the game for as long as you'd like, if you want."

"Thank you," I said, trying to sound happy despite the fact that I felt like absolute crap.

The download finished, and as Evan began to set up the game and create a character, walking me through the entire process, I felt my phone buzz in my pocket.

I was genuinely interested in the game after seeing how it began, so I waited until there was a lull in Evan's demonstration before I checked my phone.

The text was from Riley: *"Are you doing anything right*

now?"

It was the first time I'd heard from her since our conversation yesterday. *"With Evan,"* I sent back. I couldn't even text her without feeling guilty.

There were several long minutes between my text and her next reply. "Is that Riley?" Evan asked me, and I nodded, unwilling to lie to him. "Can you ask her to call me tonight? I just wanna check up on her."

"Sure."

Riley's next text said, *"Should I stay home?"*

I swallowed hard, fingers hovering over the phone screen as I tried to figure out what to say. I couldn't help but want to see her. At last, I typed out: *"I can't be around both of you at the same time right now. Come over later."*

"You start off at this city," Evan was explaining when I finished. "And you can decide what kind of magic you want to learn. I like playing as an elf who specializes in fire magic. But you can be a human water mage too; I've done a playthrough like that and it was pretty fun. But fire's definitely the coolest, I think."

"Ok," said Riley's text. I didn't reply.

"Evan?" I asked as I set my phone aside and tapped his arm to make him look at me.

"Hmm?" he replied, and then grew serious when he saw my face. "What's up?"

"I just..." I felt a lump in my throat and tried to swallow it down. "I love you, and... I hope we're friends for a long time. I don't want to fight anymore."

He smiled down at me, then wrapped an arm around

me and pulled me closer. "Never again," he agreed, kissing me on the top of my head, and I blinked back tears before he could see them.

Chapter Eight

Riley came over an hour or so after Evan's departure. Initially, seeing her after our last conversation was like meeting a stranger. I didn't know how to act around her or what to say. I wasn't even sure if being alone in my room together was a good idea.

But Mom insisted she stay for dinner and even suggested she spend the night, probably in an effort to fix whatever she thought was the cause of Riley's sad departure after her previous visit. I knew that trying to get Riley out of it would make my mom suspicious, so we were both just sort of forced to go along with the suggestion.

Nicole, as I eventually noticed, looked strangely amused throughout dinner for some reason. She'd been a little weird around Riley since her party, and I'd never thought to ask why until that night. But that would have to wait.

I retrieved pajamas for both Riley and myself, and right around the time I was taking my shirt off I realized that I'd been changing in front of her for years. I glanced over at her to see that despite her refusal to look at me, her cheeks were red, like she knew exactly what I was thinking. I hesitated. Was it right to act like nothing had changed? Were we going to address that things *had* changed? Who was in charge of deciding any of this?

Finally, I turned away and reached for my shirt, and the rustling sound behind me told me that Riley'd elected to follow my lead. I'd seen her in a bra plenty of times over the years, but now I wasn't sure if I was allowed to look. Or if I should.

I heaved a sigh, fed up. "Can we not do this?"

"Do what?" she asked and then immediately caught my exasperated look. "Sorry. I know."

"We've been friends for over a decade. This shouldn't be any different." She didn't reply, and I pressed, "Right?"

At last, she shrugged her shoulders. "That seems kind of naïve."

"It's not," I argued instinctively. "We're friends."

She held back an eye-roll and then tossed her pajama pants onto my bed. Then she turned and headed straight for me.

"What are you-?" I started to ask, but she stopped right in front of me, less than a foot away, and reached out to take my hand in hers. The tension was immediate.

I avoided her eyes for fear of what I'd do if I didn't.

She raised our joined hands, shot me a knowing look, and then plucked the pants from my other hand and walked back to the bed. "I'm more legs and you're more torso, and you gave me the shorter pants. These fit me better." She tossed me the pajama pants she'd left on the bed, and I barely reacted quickly enough to catch them.

"You've never cared that much before," I mumbled.

"Never had to prove the existence of sexual tension," she replied. "Pants happened to be a good way to do it."

I felt my face heat up. "Why are you so relaxed? You don't act like..." I trailed off, and she turned to raise an eyebrow at me.

"What, like I've been pining away for you for years? I'm still me. Same old Riley. Sass is my first language."

"I don't feel like the same person," I said. "I feel like a stranger. Like I don't even know myself."

"I know." Riley turned back to me, shooting me a sympathetic look. "I went through it."

"When?"

She hesitated and put her back to me to change into her pajama pants. I tried not to stare. "When I was twelve. That's when I started to wonder, anyway."

"But that was so long ago," I marveled. "I mean, back then I was just getting my first boyfriend."

She sighed, as though I'd said something stupid, and then turned to shoot me another knowing look. I realized what she was trying to tell me, and felt a strangely pleasant fluttering in my stomach even as my face warmed all over again. "Oh. Correlated. Got it."

"I got good at hiding the jealousy," she admitted. "Until Josh. Until it was serious."

I busied myself with changing my own pants as Riley moved to get under the covers. The fluttering feeling in my stomach intensified. I hadn't been able to completely wrap my head around what my conversation with Riley the other day had meant, but now it was finally starting to sink in.

Evan wasn't the person her future eighty-year-old self would tell her grandchildren about. *I* was that person. Or at least I could be. She'd loved me since age twelve. She'd spent years listening to me talk about my various boyfriends. She'd heard every tiny detail and had smiled through all of it just for my benefit.

I watched her sit on my bed, with everything below her waist hidden under the covers and two pillows propping her up into a sitting position. Her phone was in her hand and she was watching me a little nervously. "What?" she asked.

"I don't know," I lied, and she bit at her lip.

"Kayla, c'mon."

"I don't know if we should share a bed," I admitted, embarrassed.

"I wouldn't do anything you didn't want me to," she promised.

"You just told me you've spent five years in love with me," I said, swallowing a lump in my throat. "And it's like... looking back now, I can see it. And it's sinking in, and... I'm not sure exactly how I feel about girls in general, yet, but with you I think it might be a shorter list than you think."

"Wait, *what* would be a shorter list than I think?" Riley echoed, confused, before I gestured to the bed and she realized what I was trying to imply. When she did, she blinked twice, surprised, and then looked away from me very quickly, focusing on her phone just so she wasn't watching me. "Oh," she said, and bit her lip again to keep from smiling despite the redness in her cheeks.

"Shut up," I shot back, feeling my own face heat up, too. Thankfully, bickering with her seemed to ease the tension a little.

"I didn't say anything!"

"You didn't have to." I stared at her for a long moment, then took a deep breath and moved to the bed, sliding under the covers beside her. I lay down immediately and reached over to click the lamp on my nightstand off. It'd been the only source of light in my room, and without it, I couldn't see Riley.

I felt her shift and then readjust her pillows as she lay down beside me. As my eyes began to adjust to the darkness, her face came into view, just a few feet in front of mine. I closed my eyes for a moment, forcing myself to think of Evan, and then rolled away from her, onto my back. I opened my eyes when I felt her arm move, and whispered a quick, "Don't."

"I'm not," she whispered back, but she pressed herself to me anyway and rested her arm across my stomach, placing her head on my chest right above my heart. I held back a shiver. We'd done things like this as friends for years, so I tried to tell myself that it was okay.

I could hear her breathing quietly in the dark for what felt like several minutes while I tried to keep my heartrate down. She could hear every beat, I knew, and so I tried my best to relax; to ignore the way Riley's hand rested against the side of my hip or the way her breaths were kind of uneven.

Thump... Thump... Thump... Thump...

The hand by my hip twitched a little, and then shifted entirely to rest on my stomach, Riley's fingers splayed out over my shirt. I opened my mouth to ask her what she was doing, but then the words died in my throat and I thought better of it. She shifted slightly against me, and then her hand moved lower and her thumb ran along my exposed hip bone.

Thump. Thump. Thump. Thump.

Again, it occurred to me to speak up. Riley seemed to be waiting for me to say something. Her index finger drew circles on my hip bone and then, when the only reaction she got from me was my faster heartbeat, her hand dragged back to my stomach. This time it slid under my shirt, just barely, and, after a pause, moved a centimeter higher. She stopped there, and I reminded myself to breathe.

Riley's voice was quiet as she asked me, "Are you okay?"

My heart was in the beginning stages of going haywire, but I was okay. I trusted her. "Mhmm." My voice came out higher than expected.

Her thump swiped across the skin just below my rib cage in a wide arc, and I closed my eyes, pulse thundering in my ears. I was sure Riley could hear it against hers, with her head still pressed to my chest the way it was.

Thump, thump, thump, thump.

Her hand slid higher and her fingertips danced across the lower half of my ribcage, then slid around to my side. She stopped there, the gentle pressure on my side pulling me closer into her.

Thumpthumpthumpthump-

Riley raised her head up off of my chest and shifted upward, resting it to the pillow for a moment. I sensed her eyes on me. Then she leaned forward until her lips tickled my ear. "Your heart's beating really fast," she whispered.

"I hadn't noticed," I breathed out, managing to sound just sarcastic enough that she picked up on it and chuckled into my ear. Her hand moved down and swept across my stomach again and I squirmed. "You're feeling me up in my bed."

"Not quite," she replied.

"Close enough." She prodded at a spot on my stomach and I gave a start when it tickled. Her laugh told me she'd done it on purpose. "Out," I hissed, and she moved her arm out from under my shirt without question. I rolled toward her immediately and she jerked away with surprise, which left her lying flat on her back. I stretched my arm out over her and twisted around, sitting up partially so that my face was hovering a good foot or so over hers. Then I stared.

My eyes had adjusted to the darkness by now, and I

could see Riley looking right back up at me, lips parted and eyes struggling to stay focused, like she knew that I wanted to kiss her. I *really* wanted to kiss her.

I exhaled deeply instead, and said, "You're with our best friend. Okay?" Then I moved away and rolled over to face away from her, putting as much distance between us as I could. I could hear her breathing for another minute or so afterward.

I never got a reply before I fell asleep, and it wasn't until the next morning that I remembered I'd forgotten to tell her to call Evan.

***

I lay in bed for a while after Riley left around noon, trying to pinpoint when exactly I'd started to have feelings for her. We'd always been close, and she'd always been my best friend. Like Mom had said, we'd been attached at the hip since age six. Still, I could never recall being attracted to any *other* girls.

But I was convinced that much like Riley's admission that it had taken my getting a boyfriend to jumpstart her sexuality crisis at age twelve, it seemed as though Riley dating her first boy had been the start of mine. There'd been no reason to question my sexuality before then because I'd been attracted to guys. Now I didn't know if I was actually attracted to girls, or if Riley was just some weird exception to the rule. Was that a thing that happened? Could I actually be straight with a single, very intense exception?

At the same time, this thing with Riley felt different than it had with guys. What if I liked her more than I'd ever liked a guy? How could I be straight if my single exception was the person I loved the most? Could I even *be* considered straight even if I only liked one girl in my lifetime, or did that automatically put me in the "bisexual" category? What if things didn't work out between Riley and me and I never liked another girl again; did that still make me bisexual?

Was it disingenuous to walk around saying I was straight because I'd liked Riley? Because what if I hit thirty and met a second girl I found attractive, and then I'd been using the wrong label for over a decade by then and had to have this conversation with myself all over again?

But the reverse was possible as well. I could start labeling myself as bisexual, and then if I only ever dated one girl – and that was assuming anything actually *did* ever happen between Riley and me – I'd look like a liar.

I groaned loudly and left my room to head downstairs. Mom was at work, but Nicole was watching television in the living room. I had an epiphany when I saw her. She was close with Grace, and so maybe they'd already had a conversation about what it meant to like girls. Maybe Nicole could help me.

"Can I ask you something?" I sat down on the couch next to her, trying not to look as nervous as I felt.

"Well, good morning to you, too," she replied. "I mean, it's like almost one o'clock, but whatever." I stared at her, and she added, "Oh, yeah, what's up?"

"Your roommate, Grace. Did she ever tell you... how she knew she liked girls?"

Nicole raised an eyebrow at me, then smirked knowingly. I tried valiantly to fight off a blush, silently praying she wouldn't ask me why I wanted to know. "You want to hear her coming out story?"

I shrugged. "Maybe. I guess. If you know it, I guess it'd be kind of interesting."

"I'll tell you," said Nicole, twisting on the couch to face me. "Alright, grasshopper, I'm gonna take you through a little workshop I'm gonna call 'How to Be a Good Ally 101'."

"Okay..." I replied, not quite following.

"Anyone under thirty who's not a total idiot is fine with gay people, obviously, but it can still be a little weird when someone you know comes out to you, because you're not necessarily expecting it. But it's important to be there for them and let them vent."

I blinked at her, processing what she'd said, and then let out a quiet, "Ohhhh..." of understanding. She didn't think I was asking for myself. She thought I was asking because of *Riley*.

I paused. Wait, Nicole knew about Riley?

"Grace always talked about... oh, uh..." Nicole trailed off awkwardly, shooting me a dubious look, and then continued, "Well, she kind of had a massive crush on her high school best friend."

"Oh," I said very very quietly.

"Yeah, um... and every time her friend even talked about a boy she'd get super jealous. Her friend had a steady boyfriend throughout high school and she... hated... the guy." She pressed her lips together and suggested, "We could stop?"

"Just keep going," I sighed out. "It's bad enough already."

"Okay... well... she'd get jealous of the guy and she didn't know why, and eventually she started dating guys too just to fit in. But I think she always knew that she was lying to herself. That's how it seemed from what she told me, anyway." She stopped there, and then shot me a sympathetic look. "So Riley talked to you?"

"It's fine," I mumbled, avoiding her eyes. "Everything's fine."

"Just be a good friend," Nicole advised me. "It'll be okay. Honestly, I feel dumb for not seeing it earlier. Grace noticed right away, and she completely lacks tact so of course she made a dumb comment about it. Riley overheard and it wasn't pretty."

"Wait, what?" I was lost now. "At your party, you mean?"

"Yeah. I mean, she's got the whole skater thing going on and she'd never had a boyfriend before Evan, and they're a totally weird couple anyway. Grace met her and thought she seemed gay and mentioned it to me, and Riley overheard and got really upset. Which kind of just made her look guiltier. Ever since then, I figured Grace was right."

"You should have said something to me. She's my best friend," I insisted.

"I didn't think it was my place. You deserved to hear

it from her and she deserved to be the one to tell you. Which I'm guessing she did, so you found out the way you were supposed to. I'm glad it worked out. You're a good friend for bothering to get advice from me. I'm glad you guys are still hanging out; you shouldn't let it get weird just because she has a crush. She'll move on."

We sat in silence for a moment, and I thought back to how Riley had been in such a bad mood at Nicole's party. That mystery was solved now.

"So Grace didn't say anything about me?" I asked her abruptly, unable to hide my curiosity. "I mean, she must've wondered if Riley liked me, right? Since she went through the same thing Riley did with *her* best friend? And if it was mutual?"

"Oh, yeah," Nicole recalled with a laugh. "She did say something along the lines of 'straight as an arrow', but that was at the end of the party, so she was a little tipsy. Though I think the assessment still stands. You're in the clear, little sis." She laughed and patted me once on the arm, then stood and went into the kitchen.

I sat alone on the couch and let out a quiet sigh, wondering how I'd missed so much in one night.

***

Evan showed up at my house two days later with tears in his eyes.

I opened up the front door to see him standing there, red-faced and shaking, and knew immediately what'd happened.

"Riley broke up with me," he told me.

I took his hand and pulled him into a hug, ashamed that this was something I'd helped put into motion, both by encouraging their relationship in the first place and by admitting my mutual attraction to Riley. "Do you want to talk?" I asked him when I'd pulled away. He nodded, and so I turned to put on a pair of shoes, then grabbed his hand again and walked silently with him all the way to the creek.

We sat in our old shelter together and Evan tore up a handful of leaves as he spoke. "I don't understand why she'd do this to me. She knew that I loved her. I mean, she never said it back... but she knew that I loved her."

"I'm sure she loves you," I said. "Just maybe not in the way that you loved her."

He forced a watery laugh. "Yeah, what a cliché. The last thing I want to hear from her is 'I love you but I'm not *in* love with you,' so at least she spared me that. Short and sweet, 'it's not working out; I don't wanna do this anymore,' done."

"That doesn't sound like Riley," I replied, confused. I couldn't envision her being that cold.

"She was trying not to cry," Evan admitted. "I don't know if that makes me feel better or worse... knowing she could hardly get the words out. Mostly it just makes me wonder how long she's been doing this just because she didn't want to hurt my feelings. Especially as crazy attached as I got." He covered his eyes with his palms and groaned. "God, I was too clingy, if I'd just let her have some space, then maybe... maybe we could've... I

144

don't know."

I looked away from him, resisting the urge to say anything. He didn't need me to sit here and dash his hopes. He needed me to listen.

"But I'm probably wrong," he admitted a moment later. "It wasn't how I thought it'd be. Riley and me."

I turned to him sharply at that. "What do you mean?"

"Well..." He heaved a large sigh. "We never really kissed after the first time on Prom night."

"Never?" I was surprised, even knowing what I knew.

"Only a peck every now and then," said Evan. "Mostly it was just a lot of holding hands and sitting close. Which was okay with me, you know, no rush. I was just happy to be with her. But I did figure that if she was as into me as I was into her we'd be doing more than that. That's part of the reason I was such an ass, I guess. Didn't wanna lose her and thought that I might."

"I figured," I admitted. "Which is why I tried not to get too angry at you. Riley's kind of your dream girl."

"Was," he corrected. "God, I'm never making that mistake again. Dating a friend. I feel like my heart's been ripped out of my chest, and I don't even know if she'll still want to hang out with me anymore. Are the three of us even still gonna be our trio anymore?"

"I'll make sure we are," I assured him. "Don't worry. This isn't going to ruin us. I actually think you're taking this really well, all things considered."

"I'm in shock," Evan decided, rubbing at the back of his neck. "And I don't like crying in front of other people, even if it *is* you. I'm sure I'll go throw up later."

145

"You're gonna be okay," I told him, not only to comfort him but also to comfort myself. I leaned into him and wrapped my arms around him, and he hugged me back with another sigh.

"This hurts so badly. I'm sorry I wasn't there for you more after Josh, when you were going through this."

"It's okay. We dated for longer than you and Riley, sure, but I wasn't in love with Josh," I murmured. "You have it worse. Trust me."

I felt Evan start to shake against me, his chest heaving, and knew he was crying again when I felt wetness on my cheek. "I hate this. I never wanna feel this again," he choked out. I rubbed his back and squeezed him tighter. I didn't know what else to do.

When I finally pulled away and watched him wipe the tears from his cheeks, I offered him a small smile. "So... does this mean we're *not* gonna make out?" I asked him. I felt the heavy feeling in my chest lighten slightly when that got a laugh out of him.

"Half the time I wonder if that kiss when we were twelve was a dream," he admitted. "But I know that it wasn't, because slobbering all over you in Madison Reed's basement would be the most random nightmare I'd ever have. I wish Riley and me could've been like us. We could've just had that silent understanding that we were never gonna be a thing."

"Should've slobbered on her too a few years ago; that might've done the job," I suggested, grinning.

He laughed. "Yeah. It would've been perfect. Three friends, no chance of any of us dating. That's what we should've had all along." He sighed and missed the falter in my smile. "But if we can get through this, we *will* have all of that. I guess that's the bright side. No more tension. We can all just be what we were meant to be from the beginning: best friends for a lifetime. I just need to focus on that, and I can get through this."

"Yeah," I murmured, nodding. He sniffed and pulled me in for another hug, and I buried my face in his jacket as my own throat tightened. "What we were meant to be."

Chapter Nine

Riley called me the next day while I was at the mall with Nicole and my mother. I was waiting for them at the food court when my phone rang, and when I saw it was Riley, I hesitated. I hadn't spoken to her since she'd broken up with Evan, mostly because I felt guilty about going behind his back at all. Our sleepover the other night hadn't technically involved cheating, but it certainly felt like it had, and I felt like I owed it to Evan to keep some distance from Riley, at least until he'd recovered from having his heart broken.

But I also didn't want to ignore Riley, so I answered the phone with a knowing, "Hey."

"Hey," said Riley. I waited for her to say more, and the silence stretched on until it grew uncomfortable. "I guess," she continued at last, "that I just wanted to call because you didn't call me, and I don't know where your head is at right now, but I wanted you to know where mine is."

"Okay," I said.

"I want you to know that I didn't, like, leave him for you or anything." She sighed. "I wish I could say this in person. Are you home?"

"I'm at the mall with Nicole and my mom. We're picking out clothes and school supplies."

"Oh. Okay." There was another long pause, and I heard her take a deep breath. "Look, I don't have any expectations. I just know that if I'd stayed with him, you and I had no chance. Maybe we still have no chance. Maybe... we'll wake up in a week and this still won't feel right because of Evan. Maybe it still won't feel right in a month from now, or a year, because of Evan, or even for some other reason. Hell, maybe you'll change your mind and decide you're straight and were just temporarily mesmerized by the purple streak in my hair." I forced a laugh and she sighed again.

"My point is that I don't know what's gonna happen, Kayla. But what I do know is that there was no chance while I was with Evan, and now maybe there is a chance, however small that chance may be. With all of that said... regardless, breaking up with him was the right thing to do, and I did it for him and for me, because we both deserve to be with someone we want who wants us back. I hope that I have that in you, but if it turns out that I don't, I'll still feel good about my decision. Okay?"

"Okay," I echoed back, my heart tight in my chest. "I

just... need time."

"I know." She paused. "I'm doing a skating thing tomorrow, around two o'clock. Will you come? Maybe... Evan could try to come, too."

I hesitated. "Actually, Evan and I have plans. We're hanging out."

"Oh," she breathed out, unable to hide the disappointment in her tone. "Okay. That's— I mean, I'm glad he wants to hang out with you."

"I am too." I looked up and saw my mom and Nicole heading toward my table. "I have to go eat lunch. I'll talk to you later?"

"Sure," she replied quietly. I bit my lip and moved the phone away from my ear, staring at her picture for a moment before I pressed the button to end our call.

***

"Left thumbstick, Kayla! No, *left* thumbstick!"

Evan leaned over, panicking, as my character, Lila, looked to her left and then to her right as the zombie ran at her, mouth opening wide and green spit dripping from its tongue. I squealed and yanked the left thumbstick to the right at Evan's urging, sending Lila hurtling to the right. The zombie rushed past and she spun around, firing wildly in the correct general direction until I was sure it was dead.

Evan collapsed beside me, clutching his chest he was laughing so hard. "Oh, man. You're really, *really* bad. Like, you need years of practice."

150

"I killed it, didn't I?" I protested, feigning hurt.

"You did," he agreed, setting his controller aside with the game paused. "But we can do something else. I know *Zombie Guts* was always, uh, Riley and I's thing."

"We can do this," I insisted, avoiding his eyes. "She's not here."

"I'm sorry I didn't invite her," said Evan. "It's just..."

"It's only been two days. You're not crazy," I told him. "She's busy today, anyway. There's something going on at the skate park in, like, half an hour."

"Oh. Well... we could go watch. I could hang back or something." He shrugged his shoulders. "It's kind of a little weird without her, isn't it? She's our glue."

"I know," I admitted. "But I'm still having fun."

"Me too." He sighed and twisted around, then leaned back and placed his head in my lap. I patted him on the head and ruffled his hair as he looked up at me. "I just wish things could be normal. I wish I could feel normal, anyway. But I don't." He paused. "You and her are okay, though, right?"

"I haven't seen her since you guys broke up," I told him truthfully. "I guess we're alright, though. It's not the same with us, either." Even without throwing in my feelings for her, I still was finding it difficult to figure out how I was supposed to act around Riley now that I was caught in the middle. I wanted to be there for Evan, but I also didn't want her to feel like I was choosing him over her. However, I *also* didn't want her to feel like I was choosing her, because that implied that I wanted to date her. And *that* decision was an entirely different beast.

I looked down at Evan and wondered if Riley and I hooking up would cost us his friendship, were we to go through with it. I knew the idea of us had crossed his mind, however briefly, and I knew that if Vanessa had dated Josh, whether it was directly after our breakup or several months later, I'd have been furious with her. There was no feasible way I could envision Evan accepting Riley and me as a couple, because if I were in his shoes, I never would. But maybe he was a better person than me. I'd always figured he was.

"What'cha thinking about?" he asked me, furrowing his eyebrows. I ran a hand through his hair again and shrugged my shoulders.

"The three amigos."

"I'll try," he promised me. "Let's go to her skating thing. I want to."

"We don't have to," I insisted, but he shook his head and sat up.

"Let's go. I'll drive."

"Are you sure?"

"Yeah. C'mon." He offered his hand to me and smiled, and I felt like crying. He was trying so hard, and here I was, debating whether or not it was morally acceptable for me to date his ex.

I took his hand and told him, "We don't deserve you."

He laughed and tugged me forward into a hug. "Yeah, I'm pretty cool."

***

The Pit had been modified since I'd last seen it. A large ramp had been placed to one side, adding at least another ten feet to the drop, and a small line of skaters had formed at the ladder that led to the top. I didn't see Riley at first, but I did see one of her friends heading toward the ramp, so I caught him by the arm and asked him, "Hey, have you seen Riley?"

"Riley?" He looked around. "Uh, yeah, just a minute ago I did. She probably went to the bathroom. She's super nervous about trying the new ramp. They just added it yesterday; the drop's freaking massive. Three guys have already wiped out trying to slow themselves down afterward. It sends you straight into a massive jump on the other side with an optional grind on the way, and the best way to handle it is to just go for it and get ready for some pretty big airtime."

"Oh, okay," I said, and he grinned and skated away.

At my side, Evan murmured, "Totally different language."

"Yep," I agreed. We stood together as the next skater dropped down the ramp and then flew across The Pit to the opposite wall. My eyes widened as he went up the wall and at least four feet into the air. When he came down, his board wobbled and then slipped out from under him. He slid across the ground on his back, then immediately curled up and clutched at it, groaning. There were several "oohs" of pain from everyone who'd been watching.

"Well, that clears it up," said Evan. "Hey, at least I won't have to deal with trying to act normal around

Riley. She's just gonna die instead."

"Hey!"

That was Riley, who'd just spotted us upon leaving the bathrooms and was now sailing over to us on her board. "Speak of the devil," Evan mumbled under his breath as she slowed to a stop a few feet in front of us and then popped her board up into her hands. She had a helmet and pads on, which was relieving.

"You came," she said to me, smiling with a sort of twinkle in her eyes that had me holding her gaze for a second too long as I grinned back at her. Then I remembered Evan was beside me at the same time that she did, and she looked to him as he forced a smile and a wave.

"Hey, Riley."

"Ev," she replied with an affectionate smile. "Hey there."

"Don't die," he advised her. "I'd be sad for like a whole week if you died."

"That's probably about six more days than I deserve," she told him, sighing.

He shoved his hands into his pockets and shrugged. "I gotta pee."

We watched him walk away together, and then faced each other when he was gone. I felt self-conscious suddenly. I'd thought I was just going to be hanging out with Evan in his living room today, so I hadn't taken as much time getting ready as I normally would've.

"He'll be okay," I said to her, and she nodded.

"I knew he would. Are you?"

"Other than being slowly eaten alive by guilt? I'm great."

"You didn't do this. I did this," she told me, and before I could argue, she added, "Anyway, I'm glad you're here."

"Evan talked me into coming," I admitted. "He doesn't seem to think it's fair for me to be caught in the middle."

"He and I agree there." She squinted at me suddenly, and pointed to just beneath my eye. "Eyelash. Want me to get it?"

"No," I rushed to say, wiping carefully at my eye. When I pulled my hand away, it was empty.

"Missed it," she said, and reached out for me. "Here."

I leaned back from her. "I've *got* it."

She frowned, and her hand fell to her side. "I'm not gonna maul you if I touch your face for two seconds, Kayla. I've had five years to practice self-control around you."

"Don't say that here," I mumbled, flushing as I rubbed at my eye again. This time, I saw the eyelash on my finger when I was done. Riley shot me a disappointed look.

"Alright." She placed her skateboard back on the ground and skated away from me without another word, and I watched her go with a quiet groan.

Evan had one thing right: things had been much simpler when we'd all just been friends.

He returned a minute or so after Riley went to go get into line by the new ramp, and as I watched her stand there, I immediately felt bad for what I'd said to her. What she was about to do was potentially dangerous, and I didn't want her to do it thinking I was mad at her.

"How'd I do with her?" Evan asked me. "It was okay, right?"

My answer was distracted. "Yeah, it was good." I glanced to him. "I'll be right back, okay? Swear."

"Oh. Alright."

I left him to walk to Riley, grabbing at her hand to get her attention. "Come," I told her, and barely gave her time to grab her board before I was dragging her away, over to the back side of the building that housed the restrooms, where I knew we'd have some privacy.

She fixed me with an uncertain look when I released her hand and turned to face her. "What?"

"I'm not mad at you," I told her. "I'm just... I have a thousand other emotions going on right now and I'm finding it really, *really* hard to sort through them." I took a deep breath. "I'm gonna spend some time with Evan to try and help him get through this. I might not see you much this week. But next weekend's our last weekend before school starts up next Tuesday. You should sleep over."

"Are you sure that's a good idea?" she asked.

"No," I replied honestly. "But I want you to."

She reached down and took my hand into hers, and I knew without looking that she was linking two of her fingers with two of mine. Her other arm came up to wrap around me, and she pulled me in for a hug, the hand holding her skateboard at my back. "I love you," she told me gently. "No matter where things go from here."

I buried my face in her neck and let out a deep breath.

"I love you, too."

***

Riley nailed her turn on the ramp and made four feet of airtime look easy. When she stuck the landing, there were several cheers from the crowd, and even Evan clapped at my side and let out a loud, "Go, Riley!"

Riley found me beside him with her eyes and beamed at me. I raised my arms into the air as I clapped, grinning back at her and then blowing her a kiss. I saw her laugh, and I grinned wider as she slowed to a stop and got off of her board.

I felt like a proud girlfriend.

***

I got my schedule for senior year several days later, on the Friday before school was due to start back up, and both Evan and Riley came over so that we could compare. It was the first time I'd seen them together truly voluntarily since they'd broken up, and though they sat on opposite ends of my living room, things between the three of us felt strangely... *okay*.

"Wait, you got Mr. Morello for AP Spanish IV, too?" Evan asked, perking up as Riley read through her schedule.

"Sí, señor," Riley replied, and Evan grinned.

"Awesome. I heard he's terrible, so thankfully I don't have to suffer alone."

"I'm *so* switching to fourth period lunch to be with you guys," I told them. "Evan, we never get classes together because I'm an idiot."

"You're not an idiot," he insisted. "You're a jock."

"That's worse," Riley cut in with a laugh, and I shot her a mock-offended look. "What? It *is*."

"*Anyway*," I replied, "let me do mine. What do we have so far? You two have Spanish, English, and Lunch together, Riley and I have Art and I'll get us Lunch, and then Evan and I will have Lunch, too. That should be it, right?"

"Should be," Evan confirmed. "That'll be good, though. But you have to actually eat at our table this time!"

"I always have classes with Vanessa," I told them. "So I'll let her know I want to eat with you guys this year. It's our last one."

"I know, right?" Riley marveled. "Can you believe this time next year we'll be moving into dorm rooms? Probably at different schools, too."

"Eh, not necessarily," Evan said with a shrug. "I want to go somewhere nearby."

"Ew, why? You could probably go Ivy League," I reminded him. "You *have* to apply to at least one."

"I don't know; I kinda wanna stay pretty local. Going off on my own is intimidating. I mean, maybe I'll be ready for it in a year, but we'll see." He shrugged again. "Could be nice to stick close to you guys. I can't imagine life without seeing you on at least a weekly basis."

"I know," Riley agreed. "I'd miss you both way too

much." She and Evan shared a look and a smile, and I felt one of my own emerge at the sight of them getting along. Then I bit at my lip and smothered it as I stared at Riley. Things between all of us were just showing signs of being on their way back to normal, but every time Riley and I looked at each other, I could tell we were both thinking about ruining it all.

"Any idea what Nicole's doing this year?" Evan asked me, pulling me from my thoughts. "Is she living in the dorms again or is she getting her own apartment?"

"Her own apartment," I told him. "But she's still living with, uh..." I went slightly red and avoided Riley's eyes. "With Grace."

"Huh." Evan tried to act casual, but I could tell he was trying not to laugh at me. I guessed maybe it was a good thing that he thought of my kiss with Grace as a joke now, given that the other option was a potentially slippery slope that'd lead to him questioning my feelings for Riley again. "Well, maybe we'll be seeing more of your new girlfriend, then."

"Shut up," I retorted hastily. Riley looked away from me as Evan laughed again and got to his feet.

"Anyway, I promised my parents I'd be home before dinner, so I gotta head out. If I don't see you guys before school starts, I guess I'll catch you at lunch on Tuesday?"

"Sounds like a plan," Riley agreed, and Evan waved goodbye to us and then moved to open the front door. It shut behind him, and I immediately collapsed backwards on the couch, staring up at the ceiling.

"I hate this," I deadpanned. Riley crossed the room to come sit at my side and reached down to brush my hair out of my face.

"Yeah, me too," she sighed out. "We should figure out what we're doing."

"It's barely been two weeks since you ended it with him," I mumbled. "We'd be horrible people."

"Maybe he'd understand," Riley proposed. "He knows what it's like to fall for his best friend. He knows you can't help it." I arched an eyebrow at her in disbelief, and she deflated. "Or maybe he'd never want to speak to us again."

"We haven't even done anything wrong," I reminded her. "We can't help our feelings. We haven't acted on them, so we haven't done anything wrong. Right?"

"You and my Bible-thumping grandfather would get along," Riley told me.

I shot her a look. "Not what I meant. There's nothing wrong with who you are, or who I... might be, or whatever. I don't have a problem with..."

"Liking girls?" Riley finished. "For someone with no problem with it, you sure have a hard time saying it."

"Because it means I was wrong about a lot of things I thought I knew about myself," I explained. "Maybe I can just like you."

"Okay. So you just like me," agreed Riley. "Now what do we do?"

I snatched at the nearest pillow on the couch and pressed it to my face. "I don't know," I groaned, my voice muffled.

"Well, let's figure out what we're *not* going to do. Rule some stuff out. Like... we're *not* going to go have fake IDs made tonight so that we can drive to Vegas and get married."

"Oh, we're not? Awesome, now everything is clear to me," I sighed out, moving the pillow away from my face to glare at her.

"That was a joke," she explained, very slowly. "I'm trying to cheer you up, because you kind of seem like you're panicking right now." She glanced to the door. "What time are your mom and sister getting home?"

"I don't know. Why?"

"Because I don't want to be in here having this conversation when they come back."

"My sister knows you're gay," I told her.

"Yeah, I figured that out pretty quickly," she replied, surprising me. "I still don't want her walking in on this, because I'm guessing she doesn't know about you."

"*I* don't know about me."

"Yes, we've established that." She took my hand and stood, then helped me get to my feet. "Let's do this in your room."

"Oh, yeah, definitely. On my bed," I sassed as she led me there. "Genius idea. I wonder which decision *you're* leaning toward making."

"Hey," she replied, offended. We entered my room and she closed the door behind her, watching me as I sat on my bed. "I'm just as torn as you are. I don't want to hurt our friend."

"So then it's decided," I said, scooting back

instinctively when she moved to join me on the bed. I tried to ignore the way my pulse quickened due to our proximity as I suggested, "We stay friends to spare Evan's feelings."

"There's a small problem with that," replied Riley, inching closer to me. I tried to widen the gap between us again, but I was already at the head of my bed and had nowhere else to go.

"No idea what you're talking about," I tried to joke, and she smiled at me like she sympathized.

"Just because we don't date doesn't mean this feeling goes away. How long does it stick around? What happens if one of us dates someone else?" She paused. "What happens if there's an eyelash on your face in public, and we get into an argument because you don't want me touching you?"

"I can fix that," I decided. "I'll get better at it."

She forced a laugh. "Yeah, right. You freeze up and get this deer-in-the-headlights look on your face." She reached for my face before I could protest, and I stilled, wide-eyed. She laughed at me as her thumb brushed my chin. "See? Like that."

My argument died in my throat and I swallowed hard as Riley seemed to lose her train of thought. She watched her own fingers as they slid along my jawline, but she didn't pull away. Her hand froze by my mouth, and she hesitated briefly. Then she reached out with her thumb and ran it slowly, gently, along my bottom lip. I stared back at her, struggling to breathe correctly, until, at last, her eyes flicked up from my lips to meet my gaze. Her thumb drifted back across my bottom lip again. I made a strange noise in my throat and knocked her hand away, then leaned in to close the small gap between us.

Riley tangled her fingers in my hair and pressed herself closer to me, parting her lips slightly to kiss me back, and I forgot what my hands were supposed to do, too caught up in the feeling of Riley's lips and my own thundering heartbeat. I felt more light-headed than I was ready for. Kissing Riley was not like kissing anyone else, not even Josh. If kissing the last boy before Josh had been the kindergarten of kisses, then Josh was around late middle school and this was Graduation Day, complete with celebratory fireworks.

At some point, we took a very brief break to rest our foreheads together, and I used the opportunity to lift my fifty-pound arms and rest them on her shoulders, hooking my hands behind her head. She moved her hands to my hips and initiated the kiss this time, much more slowly and with just the slightest tilt of her head, and I lost track of time, certain I'd be content to just kiss Riley until we died from dehydration, starvation, or lack of sleep. I couldn't recall which would come sooner.

She pulled away from me first, a little out of breath, and rubbed her nose back and forth against mine affectionately. I kept my eyes closed as she pressed her forehead to mine again and murmured a quiet, "Hey."

I had to swallow a few times before I found my voice. "Hey."

She chuckled quietly and tilted her head up to kiss me again, just for a second this time. "That was really nice," she breathed out at last, once she'd pulled away. Her hands left my hips and she wrapped her arms around me, urging me closer until I could feel the warmth of her body against mine.

I let out a breath, mind still buzzing. I didn't know what to say, but then I remembered I'd been the one to kiss her first, and so I mumbled a quiet, "Whoops."

Riley dissolved into giggles and buried her face in my neck, and I found a dopey smile spreading across my lips despite myself. Riley didn't giggle. Ever. Not since we were kids.

I shrugged my shoulder in a silent message for her to sit up, and she did, leaning away from me so I could get a good look at her. Her lips were swollen and I stared as they formed a gentle smile. Her eyes were practically twinkling when I looked into them.

"You're really very pretty," I told her, flushing, and then pulled her closer again.

"You too," she mumbled, cupping my face in her hands and kissing me again for a moment. Then, breathless once again, she added a gentle, "Okay," and leaned away from me to look into my eyes. I had to blink a few times to bring myself back down to earth. "What do you think we should we do?" she asked me, licking at her lips, and we stared at each other for several seconds.

She cracked first, biting at her lip to try to keep from smiling, and I laughed openly at her, then felt awful for it and raised a hand to cover my mouth.

"Okay, yes, that was a dumb question," she admitted, pulling my hand away from my mouth. "But seriously.

What's next?"

"I don't know," I complained, running a hand through my hair. "Can't we just... make out for a few more hours?"

"If we lacked consciences, we could make out every day for the rest of our lives. But we're only awful people, as opposed to downright evil ones."

"He's gonna kill us," I realized, my heart dropping into my stomach. "He'll never forgive us."

"Maybe you're underestimating him," Riley offered, sliding her fingers through the spaces between mine and resting our joined hands on her lap. "Maybe he just needs time."

"So we just sneak around?" I asked. "That's worse than the plan we had before."

"We didn't have a plan."

"We sort of did," I insisted. "Our plan was to choose between dating openly or waiting for him to get over you. Now apparently our choices are to date openly or to date in secret."

"I do kind of prefer the second set of choices," Riley admitted, though she looked guilty as she said it. "But that's completely selfish and I know it."

"We aren't thinking clearly," I told her. "This is literally the worst time to make a decision."

"I know," Riley sighed.

"You didn't cheat," I pointed out. "We waited. We did the right thing."

"Then why doesn't it feel like it?" she mumbled. "I mean... it feels right, of course, but it feels wrong, too."

"Because we don't have his permission."

"We shouldn't have to ask. I don't think we have to ask," said Riley, but she looked dubious. "Right?"

"I don't know. I don't *think* so. But maybe we'd feel better if we did."

"And until we get the courage to do that?" she asked me.

I bit my lip and stared down at hers. They were so swollen. I wanted to kiss them again. "I am *definitely* not responsible enough to make that decision."

She scoffed. "Well, neither am I."

"We could be logical," I suggested, and then glared when she looked like she wanted to laugh at me. "Seriously. Say we're telling Evan about us, and we're asking if it's okay, and he's really furious and totally hates us and isn't okay with it. Does it make a difference if we made out once and then held off for a little while, as opposed to having been hooking up the whole time?"

"If he's gonna totally hate us, then probably not."

"What if he's a little hurt but is considering trying to accept it?" I offered. "Does it make a difference then?"

"...No?" Riley guessed. I arched an eyebrow at her and she mumbled, "Yeah, maybe."

"So... we hold off, then," I declared half-heartedly. "And so when we tell him, we can just say we had a thing at one sleepover. And..." I trailed off and then realized, "And if we word it *that* way, the whole sleepover's kind of already covered, right?"

"Totally." Riley nodded emphatically. "We already screwed up tonight. This whole night could be, like, one big encounter. We could just... not mention how long we kissed for."

"Mhmm." I hesitated, staring at her lips again and swallowing hard. "And how long would we be waiting for after this?"

"A couple weeks?" Riley guessed, and then grimaced. "...A month?" She paused again. "*Two* months, max?"

"Better get it all out tonight, then," I decided, and Riley was already nodding furiously and tugging me forward by my shirt as I leaned back in to press my lips to hers.

Chapter Ten

Vanessa slid into the desk next to me in third period English Lit on our first day back at school, her skin a shade darker than it'd been when she'd left for France.

"Hey!" she greeted me, smiling widely.

"Oh my God. Europe was good to you," I told her. "Your tan looks great!"

"It's full-body," she whispered to me with a smirk. "My uncle has a fenced-in backyard, so every time I was home alone I took advantage. You should see how dark my ass is."

"Did you meet any cute boys?" I asked her.

"Hell *yes*. It's France; of course I did. None I'm keeping in touch with now, but I definitely had an eventful summer." She shot me a curious look. "How about you? I'm sorry I had to leave you here; I bet it was hell with your friends hooking up the whole time."

"It actually wasn't all that bad," I told her. "And they broke up."

"Oh? Well, good. I just hope they're over it, because you do *not* need their drama on your mind while we're trying to get a squad together this year. I'm excited. You know we're shoo-ins for co-captains, and I hear Danny Romano is going to be our new quarterback this year." She sat up straighter but kept her voice down as she told me, "You and I are both newly single, and it's our senior year, so I propose we land dates with as many senior members of the football and basketball teams as we can this year. Starting with Danny."

"Uh," I began and laughed a little when she raised an eyebrow at me, "I think I'll leave that to you. I've had enough jocks to last a lifetime."

"But the whole point is to make Josh jealous. He might meet girls in California, and you want him to remember what he lost, don't you?"

I shrugged my shoulders. "Not really. I've kind of moved on."

"With who?" she pressed immediately, and I laughed again.

"What's with the third degree? Who says there has to be someone else?"

"Because everyone knows how the saying goes: the best way to get over someone is to get under someone else. I *know* you didn't just sit back and spend your summer alone while your friends were all over each other."

169

"I spent some time with my sister when they got bad, but I actually hung out with them for most of it," I told her. "It wasn't as bad as I thought it'd be. *And*, for the record, I never had sex with Josh, so throwing myself into bed with someone I hardly knew wasn't exactly Plan A when I wanted to try and get over him."

"If you say so. I've found it's the best approach." Vanessa shrugged her shoulders and leaned down to retrieve a tube of lip gloss and a small mirror from her purse. "I hear our teacher's cute," she told me.

"Cool." I didn't know what more she expected me to say.

"So if there's no one," she suggested, "then you can help me with Danny."

"How?" I asked, apprehensive. I didn't want to tell her that technically there *was* someone, because then she wouldn't rest until she got it out of me. But I didn't want to accidentally find myself roped into some ridiculous date plan, like I was certain I was about to be.

"He's going to ask me out, and when he does, I want to suggest a double." And *there* it was: a ridiculous date plan. "So I need you to come with us."

"What if I don't like the guy?"

"You don't have to. You just have to play wingwoman. Make sure things go well for me and Danny. Then I'll handle the next one alone, and you never have to go out with your guy again if you don't want to. Plus, you get a fun night and a dinner out of it." She closed her mirror and put it away, along with the tube of lip gloss, and then shot me a smile. "Sound good?"

"I guess," I agreed half-heartedly. I wasn't sure how to get out of it without either upsetting Vanessa or telling her the truth. There was also a good chance that telling her the truth would upset her anyway. She probably didn't *hate* gay people, but that didn't mean she'd be celebrating the fact that I was interested in another girl, especially given that it was Riley. It was already shocking enough that she didn't judge me just for being *friends* with Riley and Evan.

I turned away from her and licked my lips, my mind wandering back to Friday night. Even just thinking about it gave me goosebumps. In retrospect, I was stunned we'd had enough self-control to stop at making out.

I daydreamed throughout the rest of the period and then parted ways with Vanessa to go join Evan and Riley at lunch. I found Evan first, and we grabbed a table and claimed three chairs at it once we'd gotten our food.

At first, I didn't see Riley, but then Evan pointed her out and announced, "Hey, there she is. With one of her guy friends or whatever."

Dylan, Brett, *whoever*, was standing by one of the lunch lines, and he and Riley were talking with trays in their hands, both of them all smiles. He said something, and Riley laughed so hard she nearly dropped her tray.

If I hadn't known what I knew about Riley, *I* might've even been jealous, and so it didn't surprise me when Evan let out a quiet huff and began to scarf down the spaghetti on his tray, shaking his head all the while.

"You okay?" I asked him as he chewed.

"I guess," he replied through a mouthful of noodles, and I waited for him to swallow before he continued, "It's always that same guy, though, you know? The other one isn't all over her like he is."

"Maybe he has a crush," I conceded. "Would that be so bad? Someone else liking her?"

"He could show a little respect," Evan retorted. "She just got out of a relationship. Moving in the second she's single is a dick move."

I looked down at my tray and picked up my fork, then nudged at one of the meatballs on top of my own spaghetti. I suddenly wasn't very hungry. "How long should he wait, then?" I asked him, trying to sound casual.

Evan shrugged. "I don't know. There's not, like, an official rule. It just seems too soon."

"You still like her," I guessed. There was no way he'd gotten over a several-years-long crush in just a couple of weeks.

"I mean, I know it's over. I'm not gonna act like I have a right to tell her who she can and can't date. But it'd still hurt to see her with someone else, and I wouldn't exactly be a fan of the new guy, you know?"

"Makes sense," I agreed, still prodding at my food. "But maybe you'll feel better in... I don't know, another month?"

"Maybe," he said, but he shrugged again.

Riley left her friend and joined us at our table, and we shared a brief smile before I had to look away for fear I'd start blushing if I didn't. I knew exactly what we were both thinking about.

"Who was that?" Evan asked her, unknowingly interrupting our moment.

"Hmm?" Riley looked confused, and then glanced over her shoulder. "Oh. You know my friend. His name's-"

"No, I know who he is, but he seems into you." Evan had a hard time hiding the frustration in his tone, and Riley frowned, her eyebrows furrowing.

"Oh. Well, I don't think he is. We're just friends."

"You can date him if you want. I wouldn't care," Evan told her flippantly. He looked down at his tray, and Riley shot me a look, clearly searching for confirmation. I widened my eyes in warning and shook my head hastily.

"I'm really not interested," she said to Evan, after I was sure she'd gotten my message loud and clear. "You and I just broke up, anyway, so even if I was, I wouldn't start dating him."

"So you *are* into him, then. You don't have to act like it's hypothetical."

"I'm not," Riley insisted. "We're *just* friends."

"Whatever."

We ate in silence for a few moments and, as if it wasn't already unbearably awkward, I temporarily lost all sense of social awareness and blurted out, "So Vanessa wants me to go on a double date with her or something."

"What?" Riley asked me, her jaw dropping and her eyes widening.

"I was just trying to make conversation," I squeaked out.

"You should go," Evan encouraged me, oblivious to

Riley's venomous look across the table. "It's about time you got to go out with someone. Do you know who she's trying to set you up with?"

"No idea yet," I muttered, avoiding Riley's eyes. "I guess we'll see."

***

"What are you doing?"

Riley cornered me after lunch in our shared Art class, looking more hurt than angry. I led her to one of the tables and we sat down together, talking in hushed whispers as other students began to file into the room.

"It's just something she mentioned to me today. It might not even happen," I insisted, backpedaling. "Don't worry about it."

"If she goes through with it, you have to find a way to get out of it."

"How?"

"I don't know. Just... say you don't feel well the night of the date."

"She'll just reschedule."

"Then tell her you're not interested."

"Tried that one already. She says I don't have to be," I sighed. "I'm telling you, it wouldn't mean anything."

"So I should go out with Dylan, then?" she asked.

"Wait, that guy from lunch asked you out?" I replied, stiffening.

"No, that was Brett. Dylan asked me out on Sunday. I turned him down."

174

"You did?" I asked quietly, unable to hold back a small smile. "Really?"

"Don't flatter yourself; I'm not attracted to guys," she countered, but when she looked away I could see her trying not to smile herself.

I nudged her to get her attention again, then leaned in to whisper in her ear, "If I have to go out with Vanessa, I'll make it up to you."

"How?" she whispered back. "In case you haven't noticed, we have a friend who was seeing red a few minutes ago over me talking to another guy he doesn't even know and who I'm not even interested in. He knows you – he *trusts* you – and I'm very much interested in you. You think he was angry at lunch today? Something tells me we haven't even scratched the surface."

"He'd never blow up on us," I told her. "He'd probably just shout a little. Or even worse, he'd cry."

"Doesn't mean I'm looking forward to it," she mumbled. "I just feel so helpless. Like, all we can do is wait it out."

"Maybe not. We could help him move on," I suggested. "Try to help him heal and stuff."

She perked up and looked at me like I'd just told her I'd gotten a perfect score on my SATs. "Oh my God. Why didn't we think of that? That's genius!" She looked around at the other students in our classroom. "We can set him up on a date!"

"I don't know if that's exactly what I was thinking," I said, but it was clear she wasn't listening to me.

"There's a cute girl in our English class. She asked

him for a sheet of paper today, you know. Who doesn't bring paper on the first day of school? I bet she just wanted to talk to him."

"Or she didn't think she'd have to write anything down today," I proposed, but that went unanswered.

"I'll talk to him about it," she decided, and beside her, I winced inwardly. Evan was a smart guy. He was going to see right through this.

***

"Riley knows I can see right through her, right?"

I sighed into my phone and told Evan, lying flat on my bed, "Probably not. She's just trying to help, though."

"She hasn't shut up about Abigail Haggard all week."

"I know."

"And the thing is, I know I overreacted at lunch on Tuesday. I regret it. Especially now that it's apparently got Riley on a mission to force me to move on. Now I'm just even more convinced she wants to go out with that guy. Why else would she care so much about me getting over her?"

"She could just want you to feel better," I suggested, but I knew that I was lying, so it felt a little futile. "Or... I mean, even if she was interested in him, so what? It could still be a combination of the two. She obviously cares about you."

"Yeah, but I don't want to go out with Abigail. I mean... not that she isn't attractive, but I'm not exactly looking for a new girlfriend yet."

"I'll tell her to back off," I promised him.

"Thanks." He sighed. "I'm glad you've been here for me. I'd have gone crazy if you hadn't been around to keep me sane these past few weeks. If I ever go off to an Ivy League school and make some big mathematical breakthrough and win an award for it, I'll totally send you the trophy."

"I think I'll settle for a mention in your acceptance speech," I joked.

"Deal."

I shifted on my bed and moved my phone to my other ear. "So I want to tell you something," I gathered the courage to say, and hoped Riley wouldn't be angry with me for it later. We'd agreed to wait to tell him we were into each other, but I'd wondered since last Friday if maybe easing him into the idea of Riley and me could make it easier for him to accept it. Baby steps, so to speak.

"What's up?" His tone was serious, like he realized I wasn't joking around with him anymore. "You alright?"

"Yeah, I'm okay." I hesitated, and then was silent for a few seconds too long, because Evan spoke up before I could.

"Kayla? Are you still there?"

"Yeah, sorry. Um. Remember Nicole's birthday? And that whole thing that happened?"

"Of course." His tone hadn't changed, and I knew that there was no going back. Before now, I'd managed to convince him that Grace kissing me was officially joke-worthy, even if it'd seemed serious when he initially saw

177

it happen. Now that I'd brought it up again like this, there was no way he'd let the topic die without having a serious talk about it first.

So rather than draw it out any longer, I just said it. "I talked her into kissing me, not the other way around. She covered for me when you caught us."

I swallowed hard when he was silent, feeling my pulse quicken the longer I waited for him to answer.

And then he asked, "Why did you lie to me?"

"Because I was scared of the truth," I said, chewing on the inside of my cheek anxiously.

"And what's the truth?"

"I guess..." Here was where the baby steps came in. "I guess I was curious. You know summer was a little weird for me, and I wanted attention. I thought I wanted it from her. I don't know."

"Do you think you're...?" he trailed off, and then amended, "You dated Josh, though, so you liked him, right?"

I let out a slow breath. "Yes, I liked Josh. But."

I paused, and Evan pressed, "But...?"

"I'm... not totally sure I can rule out liking girls."

"Holy crap, Kayla." He sounded excited, but I knew it wasn't in the way it might've seemed, coming from a boy. He was just genuinely happy for me. "So you might be bisexual?"

"I think so. Maybe." I hesitated. "Probably."

"Who else knows? Does Riley know?"

"Yes, but you're the second to find out," I told him.

"When did you tell her?"

178

"Um, Friday. When she spent the night," I lied. I couldn't tell him that she'd found out practically right before she'd broken up with him, because I was certain he'd connect the dots if I did.

"You know, I wondered!" he marveled. "After you and Grace. Because you were really into it. I told you I wondered! And I was right!"

"Yeah, yeah," I deadpanned, unable to hold back a smile. "Pat yourself on the back."

"Oh, I will." I could hear the curiosity in his voice growing, and so it didn't surprise me when he bombarded me with questions. "You have to date a girl now, you know that, right? I mean, it's practically a rite of passage. How did it happen, though? I mean, did you just go all Katy Perry with Grace and then feel something? Are you into anyone? I mean, not Riley obviously, because that'd be weird and gross. I still can't believe I got paranoid enough to go *there*. But that Vanessa girl you hang out with is cute. Oh, is that why you're going on that double date with her? To cock-block that guy she likes?"

I swallowed hard, my heart settling somewhere in my stomach. "Um. No, Vanessa's just my friend. But maybe I'll date a girl. I don't know. I just wanted to tell you so you knew."

"Well, I appreciate it. Oh! I just realized we can talk about girls together now! That's gonna be cool. Hey, do you think Jenna Coleman's hot? That's the girl that plays the Doctor's companion on *Doctor Who*. Or what about Zoe Saldana? We gotta compare types sometime."

"Oh, um... yeah, I guess." I shook my head, squeezing my eyes shut. "Look, I really should go. I haven't showered yet. I'll see you at school tomorrow?"

"Yeah, sure. I won't say a word to anyone, of course."

"Thanks. Bye."

I hung up and heaved a sigh, too disappointed to even make the effort to set my phone back down on my nightstand.

"Weird and gross," I echoed Evan's words, feeling sick to my stomach. "Great."

Even worse, I now had to sit on my bed and text Riley an update of everything that'd just happened. She called me a few minutes later and said, "I can't believe you told him."

"Are you angry?"

"No, of course not," she insisted. "I'm really happy for you. And I'm glad he took it well. I mean, I wish I'd gotten a heads up, but that part was your secret to tell. And I'll act like I didn't know until last Friday."

"But it didn't help us like I thought it would," I admitted. "It actually might've made things worse."

"Well... maybe that's okay," Riley decided. "Sometimes love can wait in exchange for a stronger friendship, right?"

"I wish friendship could just coexist with love without anyone having to wait for acceptance," I mumbled.

"That's probably how Evan felt about you all summer," Riley pointed out.

"Yeah," I conceded. "But he still got to be with you. Well, theoretically. The whole lesbianism thing kind of threw a wrench in that plan. But he got to hold your hand. *I'd* like to hold your hand."

"We hold hands," she pointed out.

"You know what I mean." I sighed, and then told her, "You know you have to stop pushing Abigail on him, right? He's not interested. At least not now."

"Yeah, I know," she agreed, though she sounded disappointed about it. "Distracting him won't work. Maybe I should just tell him I'm gay."

"That's an awful idea. Please be kidding."

"Relax. Yes, I was kidding. His ego would be obliterated and he'd also immediately know we've been making googly eyes at each other behind his back."

"Gross," I laughed out, but I was thankful for the attempt to cheer me up.

"It's not. Not really," she said. "He just has to get used to the idea. Which will take a while after we come clean. But eventually it'll be okay."

"What if it isn't?" I asked her.

"It has to be. Because I've decided that I won't let it not be. He can think what he wants of me, but I won't let him blame you for this."

"That's kind of romantic," I said, smiling into the phone. "Do you treat all of your conquests like this?"

"Mhmm. All one of them."

"Evan's right," I decided. "We're totally weird and gross."

Riley laughed, and then I heard her kiss the air. "Muah! Alright, I'm going to bed. Wish me sweet dreams; last night I dreamt I skated down a ramp that stretched all the way up into the clouds. On the way down I was worried about dying, but plot twist: I lived, and at the bottom, Dylan and Evan were fighting over who was going to marry me and you were off making out with Josh."

"You did not dream that."

"I did! Swear. You don't get nightmares about us being with boys? Must be a gay thing."

"I get nightmares about showing up to cheerleading practice naked," I laughed. "Like normal people."

"Funnily enough, that's actually one of my good dreams of you."

I scoffed and rolled my eyes at my phone. "You're hilarious. Goodnight."

"Night!"

I hung up and tossed the phone onto my bed with another laugh and a shake of my head, unable to get rid of my smile. Girlfriend or not, Riley could make me happy like no one else could.

I stood and headed into the bathroom to take a shower, pausing in front of the mirror to give myself a quick once-over. I look nearly identical to how I had on the night of my junior Prom – before the addition of the heavy makeup and the changes to my hair, of course – but on the inside, I felt totally different.

I kind of felt more like me.

Chapter Eleven

Now that Nicole was back in school and living with Grace, I ate dinners alone with my mother on nights she wasn't too tired to cook after work.

Telling Evan that I liked girls had put the idea into my head to tell my mom and my sister, but I had reservations about both of them. With Nicole, I knew she'd immediately guess that there was something going on between Riley and me, and I wasn't sure I was ready for that to come out yet when we were trying so hard to keep it airtight until we told Evan. Additionally, she'd want to know how I'd figured out I liked girls and would insist on me not leaving out any details, so she'd probably get the kiss with Grace out of me eventually. And I didn't want to potentially screw up their friendship.

With Mom, my reasons were simpler: I just wasn't sure how she'd take it.

I suspected she wouldn't be completely horrified, given that Nicole had mentioned Grace's girl drama in her presence and that hadn't been an issue. But my mom was the kind of mother who'd go on and on about how perfect my wedding was going to be and about how she couldn't wait to have grandchildren. She'd mourned my relationship with Josh a little too much for me to be totally comfortable with telling her there was a pretty large chance I wouldn't be dating any boys again for a while, if at all. And sure, she still had Nicole, but I was the youngest. Her "little girl".

Riley was experiencing a similar dilemma. I met her down by the creek one evening, and we talked about it while Evan was on his way. We'd all agreed to bring our backpacks and work on our homework together, like we'd used to in middle school. We weren't in all of the same classes anymore, obviously, but it still felt like a good opportunity to get the work done without it feeling like such a chore.

"You know how my mom is." Riley sighed and rested her head against the trunk of the tree we'd built our shelter up against. Her Calculus book rested, open, on her lap. "She was devastated enough when I told her I didn't want to go to church anymore. I've been avoiding telling her for years. Partially because I was hoping I could find the 'right guy' and avoid it entirely, but given that there isn't a right guy, it's kind of inevitable at this point. And you know my dad's a total pushover."

"Maybe they'll both surprise you," I offered. "I mean, I wouldn't have guessed Nicole was cool with living with a lesbian, but look at her now."

"She's not old, though. And she's in college. Back when *our* parents were in college, I'm pretty sure schools were still segregated."

"They're not *that* old."

"Feels like they are," she mumbled. "And anyway, why does coming out even have to be a thing? People don't have to come out as red-haired, even though *that* isn't super common either."

"Well, red-haired people are visibly red-haired, and they also aren't discriminated against."

Riley scoffed. "Uh, not true. Gingers don't have souls? Also, there are totally people that are visibly gay. Like me. Otherwise Grace wouldn't have called me out."

"You are *not* visibly gay," I told her. "You're, like, the perfect amount. Gay people can tell you're gay and straight people are clueless. That's perfect."

She sighed. "Well, I'd rather be invisible."

I glanced over at her with a smile, then went back to skimming the second chapter of my Statistics textbook. "Anyway, the point is, hair color isn't an appropriate metaphor, and people have to come out because it teaches *other* people that they need to be careful who they hate because it could be someone that they love."

"Kayla dropping some knowledge. Nice."

I twisted around hastily at the sound of Evan's voice to see him jogging toward us, a grin on his face. I relaxed when I realized he'd only caught the last bit of our conversation. "Hey!" I called out, a little too brightly. "What'd you bring?"

"Calculus."

"Looks like we're all doing math," said Riley. "Me too."

"Too bad we aren't in the same class or we'd have the same assignment," Evan replied. I scooted over so that he could slide into the shelter next to me, and wound up with both my knee and shoulder pressed up against Riley's. "Not a bad first couple of weeks, though, right?"

"I wish they wouldn't dump so much homework on us right off the bat, but yeah, I like my classes," I admitted.

"You guys doing cheerleading tryouts yet?" he asked me. "I saw a poster that said they start on Monday in the hallway this morning."

"Why? Interested?" I joked.

"Not exactly. It's just that you're gonna get busy once those get going, and we probably won't see you around as much."

"I'll make time this year. Last year I had Josh, and this year I... just have you guys," I said quickly, and felt Riley dig her elbow into my side in warning.

"Good, because I don't know how we'd hang out without you. I can't stand being alone with Riley." He said this with a grin, and looked past me to Riley, who rolled her eyes in response.

"Oh, whatever. You're just worried you'll have to start getting your ass kicked on *Zombie Guts* again now that you've gotten used to beating Kayla over and over."

"I'm nicer to her than that," Evan insisted. "We do the co-op campaign most of the time."

186

"Don't lie to me. She tells me stories."

"*She* lies to you!"

"Evan, solve this for me," I cut in. I'd only been half-listening to them while I scrutinized problem number five in my statistics book.

"Wait... where's your calculator? You know you need it for this, right?"

"Are you serious? It's back at home."

"Don't worry. I've got one in my bedroom," Evan told me, already getting to his feet before I could protest. "It's closer than your house. I'll be right back."

"Thank you," I said, grateful.

"No problem."

He set his book down and jogged away, and I watched him go until I felt Riley rest her head on my shoulder. I turned to look down at her, then placed my head on top of hers and closed my eyes, just relaxing with her for a moment.

"Even after we tell him," she sighed out, "we still can't do this in front of him."

"So then what changes between us?" I asked her.

"Probably just what we do when we're alone. We could change that *now*, if we wanted, though. If we could stop feeling so badly about it." She reached for my hand, which rested palm up on my thigh, and brushed her fingers along mine, her hand hovering just over my palm. "I want to kiss you again," she admitted.

"So let's tell him," I said, half-heartedly. "When he gets back."

She moved her hand away and lifted her head,

frowning to herself. "I can't. He'll know my whole thing with him wasn't what he thought it was."

"And he'll know that I was having conversations like *this* with you at the same time that I was trying to console him after you broke up with him. But those things aren't ever going to be things he'll be happy to hear, and I'd rather he hear them from us on our terms before he shows up in the middle of a conversation we didn't want him to overhear, or... catches us the next time we slip up and start kissing. Isn't it better that we sit him down and save ourselves the risk rather than waiting around for a perfect time that'll probably never come?"

"I know that you're right," she conceded. "I just wish you weren't."

"Imagine how much better we'll feel to just have it all out there. We can tell our parents and I'll tell my sister before we tell him. Because once we tell them, we'll practically have no choice but to tell him, too, given that he's over at our houses all the time anyway."

"Okay," she breathed out. "Yeah. Let's just do it."

"By next weekend, he'll know," I decided. "They'll all know." I paused. "I just... probably have to wait until Monday to figure out exactly what I'm gonna say."

"Why? Are you busy?" she asked me, and then froze, scowling at me. "*Seriously*? That's this weekend? I thought you said *next* weekend."

"Vanessa moves quickly," I sighed. "Or Danny does, I guess. Whatever: someone asked someone out and it didn't take long for it to happen. It's tomorrow night. You should come over tomorrow and help me get ready."

"Ew."

"I'll kiss you," I offered.

"I thought that wasn't allowed."

"If we're telling Evan within the week, maybe we can let it slide one or two more times," I decided.

"Hmm." She bit her lip and looked away from me, then began to flip through her Calculus book. "Well... maybe I'll come over, then."

***

"Why are you having me do this?"

"Because I know you struggle with it and it amuses me," I said, grinning up at Riley from my spot on the stool in my bathroom as she squinted hard at me. She was concentrating on spreading an even coat of lip gloss across my bottom lip.

"You could do it yourself." She pulled away and I rubbed my lips together.

"I like seeing you do it. Remember when I did it for you on Prom night?"

She forced a laugh. "Uh, yeah. Very clearly, actually."

I stared at her as she moved away, my eyebrows furrowing as I took in the way she couldn't quite look back at me. "Oh my God. You were totally into me!"

"Obviously? We kind of established I had a really embarrassing perma-crush on you."

"Yeah, I know, but I don't mean it like that. You zoned out. I remember you zoning out because I did too, kind of!"

"You did not," she argued.

"I mean, not exactly, but I definitely remember checking out your lips."

"So I had to get all dolled up for you notice me," Riley said, scoffing, but I knew she was kidding. "I see how it is."

"I had to get a boyfriend for you to notice me," I pointed out.

"I was *twelve*! And what do you call this summer, anyway? Because I call it me having to get a boyfriend for *you* to notice *me*."

"A little hypocritical," I teased.

"Yes, you are," she countered, examining the tube of lip gloss still in her hands. "Oh, hey, it's the same one you put on me, too. It kind of tasted like strawberries in that artificial sort of way, from what I remember."

I puckered my lips at her and gave her an over-exaggerated wink. "I could refresh your memory, if you'd like."

She laughed and set the tube aside. "Gross. If that's the best game you've got, it's no wonder you're a virgin." I gaped at her and she feigned apathy, examining the spread of makeup on my bathroom counter. "What should I do next?"

"Don't make fun of me; you're a virgin, too."

"I was kidding! You're adorable." She picked up a random powder and asked, "Want this on your eyelids?"

"It's foundation, so no."

She groaned and tossed it back onto the counter.

190

"How do you keep up with all of this crap?"

"How do you stay on a skateboard for longer than two seconds?" I asked rhetorically, but Riley answered anyway.

"Practice." She grabbed a black pencil and offered it to me. "How about this?"

"That's eyeliner."

"Do you want it?"

"Sure. You can put it on me if you promise not to poke my eye out."

"I can make no such promise." She offered it to me, but I grabbed for her free hand instead and pulled her toward me.

"Try it. I gave you a pass when we were just friends, but if you're going to be my girlfriend, you'll have to learn to help me with my makeup. And I'll help you with yours."

"That's not a fair trade," she said, laughing. "I just wear that liquid skin-clearing stuff my mom forces on me, and only sometimes. But alright. Just because you called me your girlfriend." She bent over, the eyeliner pencil in her hand, but I stopped her.

"Let me stand up. It'll probably be easier if we're at the same height. Just put a little on my waterline. I'll fix it up when you're done."

"Excuse me, your what?"

"Here," I said, grinning and pointing to the correct spot while she watched.

"Yeah, okay. I'll try."

She moved in closer until she was nearly pressed

against me, then tried to find a good angle for a moment before she finally rested the outside of her hand against my cheek. She looked into my eyes and I hid a smile, then joked, "Feel the sexual tension yet?"

"Shut up," she mumbled, furrowing her eyebrows in concentration. "Or I'll blind you."

"Mmkay. If that's what you *really* want."

"Shut up," she repeated, sounding more aggravated this time, but she was also fighting off a smirk. I moved my hands to rest them on her hips and she immediately leaned back, scrutinizing me with suspicion. "You were never gonna let me do this, were you?"

"You could blind me," I told her. "So not worth the risk. I just wanted to see if you would."

She huffed and tossed the pencil aside, then leaned in and gave me a kiss I knew was meant to be quick, because after only two seconds she started to pull away. I tightened my grip on her hips and she took the hint, wrapping her arms around me and grinning against my lips.

"Honey? Your d-!"

Riley pulled away from me as soon as we heard the first syllable, but it was too late. I cringed inwardly, even as we both turned to look at my mother, who'd barged into my bedroom and was now staring into the bathroom at us from where she stood beside my bed. Her eyes were wider than I'd ever seen them and she was frozen in place, her mouth still open after she'd cut herself off mid-sentence. "D..." she started again, and then stared at us some more before she managed, "date is here, I'm sorry, did I just see what I thought I just saw?"

Riley looked over at me, panicked, and I opened and closed my mouth for a moment, struggling for words. "I, um." I swallowed hard and glanced between Riley and my mom, and then squeaked out, "Yes?"

"Maybe Riley should go home for the night," said Mom, taking several seconds to find words after my response. When nobody moved, she added, pointedly, "Goodbye, Riley."

"Goodbye, Ms. Copeland," Riley replied hastily, and then added quietly to me, "Bye, Kayla."

"Bye," I barely got out. I cleared my throat as I watched Riley go, and felt my face heat up as my mom closed the door behind her. When she turned back to me, she motioned for me to come sit on the bed. I was too flustered to do anything but obey.

She joined me, and we sat together in silence for a moment, until, at last, she took a deep breath.

"We're just going to be frank about this, okay?"

I nodded wordlessly.

"So." She paused, seemed to gather herself, and then asked, "Are you... confused?"

I shook my head very quickly, and she didn't seem to know how to respond to that.

"Well... so then you're...?"

I shook my head again as she trailed off.

Her eyebrows furrowed, and now she looked confused herself, before it dawned on her and she asked, disbelievingly, "*Both*?"

I nodded enthusiastically, relieved she'd gotten it so

quickly.

She still looked dubious, and I saw her glance to the closed bedroom door. I realized that Vanessa and the guys were probably waiting downstairs. "At the *same time?*" she clarified.

I took a deep breath, and then admitted, "The date is for Vanessa."

She shot me a stunned look. "*Vanessa,* too?"

A series of coughs overcame me, and I sat there for a moment, unable to speak until it passed. "No! Oh my God. I meant that the date is only happening because *she* likes a boy. I'm just keeping them company. I'm not interested in my date."

"But you were interested in Josh," she confirmed.

"Yes..." I said, leadingly.

"And Riley was interested in Evan."

"No." I shook my head.

"But she's... and *you*... you two are-?"

"Mhmm," I said quickly. "You're all caught up. Can I please go?"

"I'm not sure." She was silent for a moment, and then added, more to herself than to me, "What would your father say?"

"Who... cares?" I tried.

"Does Nicole know?" she asked.

"No."

"Any why not? She's your sister!"

"I was gonna tell her eventually!" I insisted. "You too! I just thought you might be upset!"

"Well of course I'm upset! I just expected-"

"-me to have your dream wedding," I acknowledged at the same time that she finished, "-you to have some respect for your friend!"

We both froze, and then she looked at me, flabbergasted. "What?"

"Oh," I mumbled, my face heating up. "You're upset because Riley and Evan only just broke up. Okay."

"You thought I had a problem with you being with a girl? *Kayla.* You know me better than that. I mean, I won't say that I'm not surprised, or that it was exactly what I had in mind when I had a daughter, but if you want to date a girl, that's fine. It's another thing entirely to do something like this to your friends, because I don't like the idea of you dating one of them after she's just dated the other. You need to think about whether or not this is worth the risk of ten years of friendship to you. And while we're at it, I really don't think that this date tonight is a good idea."

"Mom," I groaned out. "I know what I'm doing."

"No, I don't think so." She shook her head and stood. "I'm going downstairs and telling them you're going to have to cancel. You are juggling enough hearts as it is, young lady. And don't think we aren't going to talk about this some more when I get back."

"Mom! *Seriously?*" I groaned out. She ignored me, and I gaped at her back as she left my bedroom and closed the door behind herself. "*Mom!*"

***

195

"Most awkward night of my life. Nothing even comes close."

"At least she was cool," Riley said on the other end of the line. "I have no idea if my parents are going to be okay with it."

"No, you don't understand," I elaborated, feeling a little nauseous. "I got a freaking modified *talk*. I don't even want to know how my mom knew so much about how lesbian sex works. I mean, it's not like she went into detail, but she knows more than I thought she did. She knew stuff I didn't know until I googled it while I was trying to figure out if I was legit into girls or just wanted to kiss you."

"Oh... wow, ew, that's traumatizing."

"As it turns out, there is such thing as too accepting. *Also*, apparently she had a ton of gay guy friends in grad school. Who knew?"

"We need to, like, take some of your mom's acceptance and suck it out of her and put it into my parents. The only thing I'm certain of is that they won't hold an exorcism or kick me out of the house. Otherwise, all bets are off. Not gonna lie, though... a part of me is glad your mom shut down your date tonight."

"Vanessa won't be happy with me."

"Why not? You couldn't help that your mom made you cancel. I bet she won't blame you."

I shrugged my shoulders, though she couldn't see it. "I guess we'll see."

Chapter Twelve

We had a test in the Statistics class Vanessa and I shared on Monday, so I only got a couple of seconds to talk to her at the very beginning of class.

"Hey, I'm sorry about last night," I told her. "Did it ruin the whole thing?"

"Don't worry about it," she replied with a shake of her head, much to my surprise. "I'll fill you in after school today."

"Alright."

I went through the rest of my day wondering what I could've possibly missed that warranted an explanation Vanessa couldn't give me in the hallway between classes. After school, we met up outside her Physics class and walked together to the gym, where we planned to meet up with the other girls from last year's squad to hold tryouts. None of us were going to have to try out, but there were newcomers who were supposed to have routines prepared. Our coach would be there to help make a decision too, but Vanessa and I, as official co-captains, would share just as much responsibility in choosing who would make it and who wouldn't.

"So Jesse – your date – and Danny and I all decided we'd go back to Danny's house rather than to dinner like we originally planned. He has this wooded area behind his house and he wanted to smoke pot, which I'm not, like, *that* into, but I didn't want to be lame so I said I'd go. And Jesse was really weird. He was already clearly not into the idea of the date before we got to your place, so you wouldn't have liked him anyway. Also, he was *way* too pretty to be straight."

"Oh?" I asked, trying hard to follow her. Her story was kind of all over the place, and I wasn't sure that it had a point.

"Yeah. Anyway, we went to Danny's and the two of them got really high and acted like idiots for a few hours. Jesse ate like ten of those mini bags of potato chips. It was really boring. Danny wanted to do another date another time afterward, but I turned him down." She shrugged. "So I guess it was kind of a bust."

"I'm sorry I ruined it," I apologized.

"No, it turned out to be a good thing. If you'd have come along, you and Jesse would've had nothing to talk about and I might've never realized Danny wasn't my type."

"I thought the idea was that I didn't have to like the

other guy?" I recalled, confused.

"Well, you didn't *have* to, but that doesn't mean I wanted the friend Danny brought along to be a stoner closet case."

"Oh," I said again. We were approaching the gym; I could see it at the end of the hallway. Worried we'd get there before I could hear more from her, I hurried to add, "Well, if he *is* gay, I hope he, like, realizes it and doesn't keep going on dates with girls."

"Right? Don't waste our time. I'll set us up on another double, though, once I actually find good guys for both of us. Next time I'll screen the friend before I set you up with him."

We reached the gym and she moved to push open the door, but I reached out a hand to stop her.

"Wait. Uh, I should tell you something."

"Hmm?" She paused and let the door close. "What?"

"I've been dating..." I started, and then hesitated and finished, "...someone. So I can't help you out with the whole double date thing."

She looked taken aback at first, and then confused. "Why didn't you say anything?"

"Because." I paused, trying to figure out how best to break this to her, if I was really going to go through with it. My mom had surprised me, so I could only hope that Vanessa would, too. "Okay, so remember that time you went out with Trent Ronsky after he'd just been suspended from the football team for having a 'C' in one class, and you didn't want to tell me even though I wound up being fine with it? And I told you that I'd support you in whoever you dated as long as he was a decent guy?"

"Yeah, but then he started talking to Tabitha Reynolds who was on the soccer team and who isn't even cute, so I decided-"

"You stopped seeing him, yeah, but that's not the point," I interrupted, stopping her before she could get going. "The point is that you were worried I'd judge you for liking him, and so you didn't tell me about it." I paused, waiting for it to click, and she sighed in realization.

"Oh, God. He's a nerd, isn't he? Is he at least cute?"

"He's a *she...*" I said carefully, and then pressed my lips together and waited for her reaction.

She smiled a little at first, like she wasn't sure if I was joking or not, and then, when she saw how nervous I looked, she shook her head at me in disbelief. "Wait, what?"

"I'm kind of seeing a girl?" I repeated uncertainly.

"Like, a female? A *girl?*"

"Yeah."

"Oh my God." She was silent for a moment, letting it sink in, and then she gripped my arm and leaned in close, gaping at me. "*Who?*"

"I shouldn't say yet," I told her.

"Do I know her?"

"Yes? Not *really...* but kind of?"

"Is she hot?"

"Well... I mean, *I* think so," I replied, a little confused at the direction this was going in.

"But, like, hotter than me? You can't date someone hotter than me."

I laughed despite myself, and she smiled back at me. I knew then that we were going to be okay. "Why not?" I asked, curious to hear what I knew was going to be a ridiculous answer.

"Because then if she hangs out with us I'll be the ugly single friend, duh. Anyway, are you, like, bi or whatever now?"

"I'm kind of new to this so I'm not totally sure how it works, but I think I kind of always *was*?"

She shrugged. "That's cool. Hey! Last question: did you ever have a crush on me? It's okay to admit it."

"Stop," I laughed out, shoving her a little, and she grinned and moved to push the gym door open again.

"I'm gonna take that as a 'yes'. You are *so* telling me more about this when we're done with tryouts. I mean, I've thought about kissing a girl because how could I not at least try it, but actually doing it seems like a stretch. How did you get the guts to go there?"

"I'll tell you all about it later, V," I replied with a shake of my head and followed her into the gymnasium.

***

Three days later on Thursday afternoon, just a few minutes after I'd gotten home from school, I found myself pacing back and forth in my room, staring down at the cell phone in my hand.

Two things were supposed to be happening now. The

201

first was that Riley was coming out to her parents. The second was that I'd been tasked with inviting Evan down to the creek to finally tell him the truth.

I stared down at the unsent text I'd typed out, trying to gather the courage to send it. *"Creek with me and Riley? Not sure what time yet but need to talk,"* it said.

The worst thing was that I couldn't even hope for a delay this evening, because the only one I might get would be caused by a bad reaction from Riley's parents. And honestly, I was so sick of coming out to people that the less of a deal was made out of it, the better.

I backed out of my text to Evan and vowed to send it in a few minutes. Evan was supposed to be the person we told last, so that we'd be so backed into a corner that we'd be literally unable to chicken out for fear that he'd hear it from someone else. Vanessa'd gotten Riley's name out of me yesterday, and she was already bursting with the urge to tell everyone that she knew, so this was it. It was happening today.

I crafted my text to Nicole carefully, and let out a slow breath and sent: *"So it turns out Riley's not the only senior girl you know who likes other girls."* I figured she'd appreciate the humor in it, and maybe she'd go easier on Grace if I just treated the whole thing lightly. Still, I was shaking a little as I sent the message.

I knew she was done with class for the day, so it didn't surprise me that I heard back from her relatively quickly, just a few seconds after I'd gone back to rereading my message to Evan.

"Grace came clean last week; already murdered her

over it and was just waiting for you to update me. Congrats, Riley's adorable. Love you! Talk now or later?" There was a smiley face at the end of the message, and I let out a sigh of relief.

"Later. You're the best," I sent back, and vowed to go visit her more this year than I had during my last. She was one of many people I'd neglected in favor of Josh. I knew it wouldn't be like that with Riley. Josh had been a separate part of my life, almost like he'd been on the outside, off on his own little island.

Riley was smack dab in the middle. Though we hadn't felt comfortable calling it official yet, I knew our transition from friends to dating was going to be seamless when it came to how I divided my time. I could only hope that Evan was still willing to be a part of the equation.

I shook out my arms and groaned aloud, then pulled up my text to him and pressed send before I could think about it any longer.

Then my phone rang. Riley.

"Is everything okay?" I asked by means of greeting.

"I'm shaking. Holy crap," Riley murmured on the other end. "Nobody hates me or wants me to date boys."

I burst into a grin. "Told you! I told you they'd be okay."

"Mom is *so* not okay, but I think she's having the grandchildren freak-out you expected from *your* mom. Dad's with her right now," she explained. "I feel like I'm in shock. If Evan doesn't hate us… if he can just be okay with this *eventually*… then we just get to do it. Just like that. It could be so easy." She paused, and then let out a long breath. "Okay, not super easy, because we'll still be two girls dating, but compared to how bad we *thought* it could be..."

"You're shaking so hard your *voice* is shaking, Riley," I told her. "Try to calm down. Deep breaths."

"I don't want to tell him," she told me, breathing hard. "He'll hate us. And we'd deserve it. Or I would, at least."

"Literally everyone that's found out this past week has been a pleasant surprise. I bet he'll be, too. We just have to do this one thing and then we'll be done with this bizarre coming out marathon thing we've kind of awkwardly been obligated to do. You told Dylan and Brett, right?"

"Brett thought it was hot because he's kind of an asshole sometimes, and he seemed like he wasn't that surprised that I liked girls. Dylan said he was happy for me even though I think he was a little disappointed," Riley admitted. "Evan's literally all that's left. He's going to hate that we told him last, too, you know."

"Maybe he'll understand."

"Maybe we shouldn't tell him he was last," Riley suggested. "Have you texted him?"

"Yeah."

"Cool. Great. I'm gonna puke."

"Deep breaths," I repeated. "I'm gonna walk down to the creek. Meet me there and we'll wait for him?"

"Okay. Yes, I'll head there in a few minutes. I'm not sure if I should stick around to talk to my parents some more; they're still in the other room. I'd like to get out of here, though."

"Let me know," I told her. "Bye."

After I hung up, I changed into a pair of sneakers and then began the walk to the creek. I thought of the day I'd gone there at age thirteen, just before Riley and Evan and I had started high school, and of how we'd all agreed that we'd never let anything get in the way of our friendship.

Back then, the threats we'd envisioned had been schedule clashes and a few new friends. We'd been worried about changes to who we were, but I knew it went without saying that when we'd vowed to not let who we became affect our friendship, we'd been talking about winding up in different social cliques or developing differing interests. So when those things had happened, we'd been able to stick it out.

This one was directly out of left field, and never in my wildest dreams would I have ever seen it coming. I never thought something as natural as falling in love would be an issue. Not when I was just trying to stay friends with two people I already knew I loved more than anyone else in the world.

I'd kissed Evan at age twelve and to this day, we joked about how awful it'd been. Maybe I should've realized right then, as Evan was drooling on me at Madison Reed's thirteenth birthday party, that if it wasn't going to be him and Riley, it was going to be Riley and me.

I wondered if Riley had realized, as she sat in Madison's basement with us and watched us kiss, who she'd been jealous of. I wondered if she was as shocked that we'd wound up here as I was. And mostly, I wondered if she had any idea what we were supposed to say, because *I* definitely didn't.

My phone buzzed with a reply from Evan: *"Sure, just tell me when. Everything alright?"*

I pocketed my phone and swallowed hard, electing not to reply. He'd find everything out when he met us anyway, and I hated that even now he was trying to make sure everything was okay with me and with Riley. I didn't feel like I deserved his empathy.

I reached the creek before Riley, expectedly, and crawled into our shelter, lying flat on my stomach and staring out at the water. I pictured a tinier, shorter Evan, ankle deep in the creek, trying to catch frogs with Riley while I ran away squealing about how gross they both were. The memory faded and I frowned.

I knew right then that Riley and I were not, in fact, a sure thing. I loved her, but I loved Evan too, and I didn't want to lose him. If his friendship hinged on Riley and me waiting longer to date, I'd agree to that in an instant. If it hinged on *never* dating Riley... I didn't want to think about how I'd make that decision. Back when he'd been dating her, choosing her over him had felt easy. But now that I'd spent so long going behind his back and feeling awful about it, I wasn't so sure I didn't owe it to him to make sure things stayed the same between the three of us.

We were the three amigos. We'd always been. I couldn't imagine doing this thing with Riley without his support. I couldn't do to him what he'd unknowingly done to me over the summer.

Riley arrived a few minutes later. I got out of the shelter and then pulled her into a tight hug when she reached me. She collapsed into my arms and squeezed me tight. When she pulled away, I sent a text to Evan telling him to come.

We sat in the shelter together as we waited, and Riley chewed at her bottom lip anxiously, her right hand fiddling with the fingers of her left.

"What do we say?" she asked me at last. "Who starts?"

"I can start," I decided. "Maybe it's better he hears it from me."

"And I just stand there?" she replied. "And just say nothing while you explain to him that I basically dated him out of desperation and pity until I broke up with him to date you?"

"You know that's not what happened," I murmured.

"That's how it's gonna sound to him!"

"Then we have to explain better. We have to explain all of it: the pressure there is to date a guy when you're a girl, that you thought maybe you could fall in love with him, that you broke up with him because it was the right thing to do, regardless of how things turned out with us. All of that. And... he could understand that all of that stuff and that how we felt couldn't be helped."

"But it's like you said before. We acted on it. *This,*" she squeezed my hand, "could be helped."

I didn't have a response for that.

Riley let go of my hand when we both heard leaves crunching in the distance. Evan came into view and waved a hand when he saw we'd spotted him.

"Hey, guys," he greeted us easily. "Oh, cool, you didn't bring backpacks, either. Wasn't sure if we were gonna work on homework again."

"No, just wanted to talk," I said, clearing my throat. There was a nervous ball of energy building in my stomach, far worse than when I'd told Vanessa or my sister or even when my mom had walked in on Riley and me. It was sending shivers throughout my body I had to reel in before they could make me tremble visibly. I understood how Riley had felt with her parents.

I stood and looked back at Riley, who was very clearly pale-faced and couldn't even bring herself to open her mouth. Evan, upon catching sight of her, asked her, "Whoa, Riley, are you sick?"

Riley shook her head hastily, glanced at him, and forced a smile. "Just feel a little nauseous," she managed. "Don't worry about me."

"You sure? I can go grab something for that from-"

"Evan," I interrupted, grabbing his arm and dragging him to the shelter, "just sit down."

"Oh. Okay?" He looked confused, but took a seat.

Riley left the shelter through the other open side and walked around to place herself somewhere behind me, a little off to my left. I watched her lean against a tree before I turned back to Evan, who had an eyebrow arched in amusement. "Why does it feel like you guys are about to tell me I have a serious problem and I need help? Is this about my video game addiction?" He paused and watched Riley and I exchange another look. Riley looked to be growing more and more mortified by the second. "And you're not laughing. That's not good."

"We have to tell you something," I blurted before I could lose the nerve. "Can you just listen?"

He closed his mouth and his eyebrows furrowed. "What's going on?"

I started to say something, but then Riley spoke up behind me and the words died in my throat. "You know how when we were dating, I... that first night was different from the rest of the time? How we hardly did anything after that first time?"

He looked embarrassed at the reminder. "That was a while back; we don't have to-"

"I was trying," Riley began, cutting him off, and then hesitated for a moment before she started again. "That first night I wanted so badly to just be normal. Kayla had Josh and I wanted to want you, because the idea of you and me seemed perfect and I knew that if I was going to be with anyone..." She took in a shaky breath. "...any *guy*, it was going to be you."

I saw the clear change in his expression as he went from confused to stony-faced. His eyebrows dropped and then pulled together, his mouth formed a thin line, and his eyes narrowed. He looked back and forth between us for a moment, visibly connecting the dots, and then abruptly got to his feet.

"I don't think I want to hear this."

"Evan-" I started, catching his wrist, but he yanked it out of my grip and glared at me.

"You knew how much I liked her."

209

"It didn't start until after you guys broke up," I insisted.

"Oh, wow, thanks. Congratulations on being only a *moderately* shitty friend. I can't believe this."

"Can you just hear us out?" I asked. He pushed past me, bumping his shoulder into mine so hard that he accidentally knocked me off-balance, and I landed on the hand I stuck out to try and break my fall. "Ow!"

I heard leaves crunching more quickly, like someone was running, and when I turned from my spot on the ground, it was just in time to see Riley press both of her hands to Evan's right bicep and send him sprawling sideways onto the ground. He landed hard, and it seemed to take a few seconds for it to sink in that she'd pushed him. When it did, he stared up at her with surprise even as she glared down at him.

"You were awful to Kayla when we were dating, and she still never told me to break up with you, even though she liked me," Riley spat at him. "And it ended with us because I realized you weren't the exception I was hoping you were, yes, but also because I didn't like who you were when I was with you. You weren't a good friend. And we've still tried hard to be good friends to you, but... I'm sorry, I wasn't going to ignore that Kayla liked me back given that I've had feelings for her since I was twelve."

Evan's jaw was tensed, and although he looked angry, when I got up and managed to rejoin Riley, I could see his eyes getting watery. She didn't stop there.

"I know that you know what it's like to feel that way

210

about someone, and I'm sorry that I couldn't return those feelings. But Kayla could, and she does, and I guess it's naïve of us, but we were hoping that you could be okay with that eventually. Because even despite how you were over the summer, we love you and we don't want to lose you. We waited this long to even *try* to make it official because we didn't want to hurt you."

He blinked and looked away from her, and then reached up to wipe at his eyes. My throat felt tight but my eyes were dry; Riley, on the other hand, had been crying openly throughout her whole speech.

"So I'm just supposed to say 'okay' and just be cool with the fact that this has been going on behind my back, and if I don't, I'm not a good friend?" he asked. "Kind of a high bar to set, don't you think?"

"That's not how it is," Riley began, but he let out a sarcastic laugh at that.

"Oh, you mean Kayla *didn't* hang out with me, listen to me talk about how broken-hearted I was over you, then go over to your house and make out with you afterward?"

"I'd never do that to you, Evan," I murmured.

"You expect me to just believe that?" he asked, turning to look at me.

"Yes," I said, and stared back at him, unwavering.

He broke eye contact first, his gaze darting down to his lap as he sniffed. "Then how did it go?" he asked at last, his tone bitter. Riley took over again.

"Deep down, I knew that I liked Kayla, and that that probably meant that I was at the very least bisexual, but

I thought that she could never like me, so I was hoping that I'd fall for a guy and then that would solve the problem. I had this idea in my head that maybe I just liked her so much because she was my best friend. Naturally, that meant that you, as my other best friend, were the best choice of a guy I was ever going to have. And Kayla was with Josh, so when you kissed me, I went with it. But then, as it went on with us over those next few weeks, I knew it wasn't the way it was supposed to be. But I didn't want to hurt you." She hesitated. "Then you told me about Nicole's party."

He shook his head with disbelief. "So the instant you found out Kayla liked girls, you dumped me."

"I found out Kayla liked *me*," she corrected. "When I went and talked to her, I found out. But I broke up with you because I was always going to have to break up with you. Whether it was in another month, or a year, or when we were married with two kids at forty years old, it was going to happen. You can't tell me that if you were in my situation you wouldn't have done the same thing."

"Then you shouldn't have dated me. You just led me on."

"I made a mistake. I should've listened to what I felt about you all along. But I didn't, and I'm sorry. The last thing I wanted to do was to take advantage of you, and I know that I did. I don't think I deserve any sort of forgiveness for that."

"Well," he began, but then swallowed hard and fell silent. Riley took a seat beside him, drained. He looked between us for a moment, and then asked, "Couldn't you have waited longer?"

Riley and I exchanged a look, and then I told him, tentatively, "That's not totally off the table. We haven't stopped caring about you."

"But then I'll know you're just holding off for my benefit. That's pathetic." He shook his head and took in a deep breath. "I can't believe this."

I sat down on the ground across from him and Riley as he dropped his head into his left hand. His right hand ran through his hair and then settled on the back of his neck, his head bowed. We were all quiet for a moment as Riley and I waited for him to say more.

It felt like minutes had passed before he finally raised his head. His eyes were watery and red-rimmed, and he sniffed before he spoke.

"I don't want to be selfish. You guys are my best friends. But can you at least just... pretend to just be friends around me? For a while?" He pressed his lips together and forced a smile, and Riley and I exchanged relieved looks. I felt like a two-ton weight had been lifted from my shoulders.

"Believe me," I said, "After dealing with you guys over the summer, I wouldn't have it any other way." I stood up and offered him my hand, and he took it carefully, then let me help him to his feet.

"I guess," he admitted to me as Riley stood beside him, "that I can't be *that* mad about you stealing my girlfriend when she'd already stopped being my girlfriend and never really liked me in the first place. I just wish you guys had figured this crap out before Prom night. I still would've been upset, but at least I'd have less of a right to be." He turned to Riley. "But, honestly, I guess it kind of helps knowing that you're gay. Means I never really had much of a chance anyway."

She smiled at him and pulled him in for a hug, which he grudgingly returned, his shoulders slouched and his smile looking more like a grimace. "I love you," she told him.

"Yeah, me too," he sighed, and then pulled back slightly to offer an outstretched arm to me. I grinned at him and joined them, wrapping one arm around Evan and another around Riley. "I have a few more requests, though."

"Okay," I said.

"The first is that you guys give me time to get used to the idea. Kind of a given." He let us go and moved away a little before he continued. "The second is that *after* that time has passed, you help me get a date with Abigail. I think she's cute, but I don't want it to just be a rebound or something I'm rushed into."

"Done and done," Riley agreed. "I already told you I thought you guys would make a cute couple, anyway."

"What else?" I cut in curiously.

He ran a hand through his hair, and then cracked the first real smile I'd seen from him. "Last, but most importantly: please, *please* don't third-wheel me."

Riley and I exchanged grins. "Deal," she echoed, and then stuck her pinky finger out between the three of us. I watched Evan as he glanced back and forth between us.

"Alright," he said at last, and lifted his arm, his pinky outstretched. He linked it with Riley's and echoed, with a disbelieving shake of his head. "I can't believe I'm saying this, but... sounds like a deal."

I looked at Evan, and one of the corners of his mouth quirked upward as he stared back at me, like he was trying to tell me that even if it took some time, we were going to be okay.

Then I looked at Riley. Just a few short months ago, I'd been worried that I was losing her, first because of Josh and then because of Evan. Now I had her for the rest of my life, if we wanted.

She beamed at me, and I grinned back, unable to contain it. We were doing this. We were *really* doing this.

"Deal," I breathed out, and reached out to link my pinky with theirs.

CPSIA information can be obtained
at www.ICGtesting.com
Printed in the USA
LVOW03s2247250318
571127LV00001B/258/P